MEET ME IN
DREAM
LAND

✦·⁺

A collection of fantasy and science fiction.

MCKAYLA EATON

DEDICATION

For my husband and for the chilly nights spent
next to you looking up at the stars.

If you are a dreamer, come in

If you are a dreamer, a wisher, a liar,

A hope-er, a pray-er, a magic bean buyer...

If you're a pretender, come sit by the fire

For we have some flax-golden tales to spin.

Come in!

Come in!

- Shel Silverstein

CONTENTS

THE NAME OF THE WOOD

An east wind slinks through the old, western hemlocks as Nora Lee walks barefoot, pale toes gracing the fallen leaves with their touch, heap of skirts and furs held up in one hand to avoid disturbing the floor of the ancient forest. The bottoms of her pale feet are turning brown, the earth leaving its footprints on her soles.

Already the ground is turning hard and cold; winter will visit early this year.

Nora Lee whistles a tune to match the wind as she makes her way through the wood along the stream side, fresh clear water running down from the peaks; cold mountain tears trickling to the valley below. Pine needles swirl in the stream, bobbing to the surface.

There is no clearly marked trail, no signs or well travelled way, but Nora Lee could not get lost even if she wanted to: she hails from a long line of women, matriarchs who spent generations taming and surviving off this wild land.

But losing her way is the least of the dangers in this wood.

There are monsters here: monsters, fairies, and spirits of the dead. Nora Lee knows these things exist because she has seen them, and her mother has seen them, and her mother's mother.

There are men who roam this wood too. They hunt the wild game and the vermin that threaten their flocks. And sometimes they hunt the monsters. But how does one tell the difference between the monsters and the men?

Nora Lee remembers asking this of her mother when she was still a little girl as they sat by the fire. Her mother began to braid her long white-blonde hair between quick, delicate fingers, as gentle and as nimble as spider legs.

"When you meet a creature in the wood," her mother had started, her voice a husky whisper, "ask it in which wood it walks."

Her mother was a wise woman: a herbalist and a hunter. A provider and a homemaker. Nora Lee remembered watching her do everything, from cleaning their clothes in the stream to butchering a deer, always with a sense of curiosity and awe. There was a longing in her to learn the ways of her mother and their ancestors.

"Don't let it trick you," she instructed. "Do not let it say, 'this wood', or 'the old wood'. But insist it says it's true name."

"Why, Momma?" Nora Lee had asked, still too young to know the dangers that filled the wood she called home. Her mother continued to braid her hair, pulling it back into a harsh, straight rope until it pulled the sides of Nora Lee's face taunt.

"Because the name of this forest is forgotten. Only creatures as old as the forest itself know its name... And those are dangerous creatures indeed."

Passing a bone white hand along the exterior wall of her cabin, Nora Lee feels the soft wood beneath her palm, a smooth, fine texture that has taken the harsh mountain winds years of wailing and buffeting to produce. It is an unremarkable abode from first glance; four walls, a thatched roof, shuttered windows, and a coop beside it. But within exists a forest niche carefully crafted over years by the steady hands and quick minds of her ancestors.

When the door shuts behind her the outside realities are banished; no wind whistles through the cracks, no cold glazes the windows with frost. There are no vermin in Nora Lee's house—never a mouse, squirrel, or songbird.

Pharaoh, her hawk, sits near the fire, on a perch carved by a grandmother Nora Lee never met. It has always stood in that spot by the hearth, though empty throughout her childhood. A hawk is a hard creature to tame, involving many sleepless nights; staying up, keeping the bird awake, staring into the eyes of a predator until you become predator and it prey. A brutal process, for a brutal animal—but pain forms strong bonds.

The hawk opens a black, glassy eye, ruffling feathers the colours of a forest fire—amber, charcoal, and gray—before returning silently to his slumber. He is a king in the wood and hunts much of Nora Lee's sustenance even in the dead of winter when things scurry and scuttle beneath hard packed snow.

Nora Lee nods to Pharaoh—he is a companion, not a pet; she never strokes him besides on the rare occasion he allows her after a kill: a small scratch along the strong line of his throat.

Hanging her bow on it's peg, she curls into her chair by the window. She pulls her feet up beneath her, cold and damp from walking the wood barefoot. She lets her white-gold locks free of their ribbons to dangle over her shoulder. The beads and feathers in her hair are heavy but remind her of the burden of the wood, and of its many blessings. She has always worn the wood in her hair just as the wood wears her footprints.

She opens the shutters. A row of clay bottles and jars lined up along the sill catch the moonlight in their polished surfaces; some are old, stamped with the fingerprints of women long returned to the earth, others new and fresh from the kiln down in the valley below.

The town has a public kiln that anyone can use for a modest fare. Nora Lee uses it often, taking her spun clay bowls, pots, and cups down in her basket and always leaving behind a little toy, a wolf or bird or bear, for the children of the village to play with.

A lazy tower of smoke spirals toward the sky and Nora Lee leans forward to peer out the window, squinting into the darkness to see the smoke rising from the homes far below. She used to journey there with her mother, walk through the cobbled streets, smell the pies baking and hear the music of penny flutes and laughing children.

Her mother hadn't liked the town's people, didn't look like them, didn't fit—and Nora Lee didn't look much like their children either. Mother had been tall, standing a head even above most of the men, and dressed in heavy leather and fur rather than the soft wool dresses which were the common feminine garment.

As a child, Nora Lee had been a gaunt girl with too prominent cheekbones and a quiet demeanor unsettling in one so young. But her reserved nature was only a cloak to her curiosity. She would stare wide eyed at the town's people with their horses and carts; their noisy forges and messy stables, and most of all she would stare at their soldiers.

"Not soldiers," Mother had corrected her more than once. "Savages. Killers, but not brave like men of War."

But Nora Lee did not know or understand War—she hardly knew or understood Men. So to her any man who carried an axe or a dagger or a bow was a soldier. And she fancied them, admired the way their weapons spoke of action and adventure, but she also knew well enough to keep her distance. They were dangerous.

"More dangerous than the bear or wolf or mountain lion," Mother had told her, "because they are rational but know not what to do with their rationality: mere beasts, clever enough to kill but not intelligent enough to know what is, or is not, good for slaughter."

Mother hated Men more than any other creature and never spoke a word more than she needed to in order to buy or sell while in the valley. Not even when the women would gather their young ones to their skirts and shuffle them indoors or when the young men with the foreshadowing of stubble on their chins would point and mumble under their breath did Mother say anything or so much as look in their direction.

Nora Lee could still hear the word, said under strangers' breath, as her and Mother passed: *witch.*

Seasons change in the mountains like the shadow of a sundial. Regular, inevitable—yet the switch from one to the other is indistinguishable. In a day—in a blink of a giant's eye—Summer has turned to Autumn, Autumn to Winter, and Winter to Spring when the young girls of the valley town shed their furs and cloaks and emerge: their chests fuller and hips wider than they were mere months before. The boys, not men yet—something in between—have shadowed jaws and forearms growing as round as tree limbs, but the coals of their dwindling youth still keep their eyes burning bright.

But it is not Spring yet. Winter is still young, and the universe still sings its lullaby to the wood, luring it and everything that lives within toward the slumber before Janus's door. Though near the age of the blossoming girls in the valley, approaching their sixteenth and seventeenth summers, Nora Lee doesn't have such changes to look forward to. Her body has long hardened, sculpted and formed by the elements. Her hips are made for climbing mountains, not bearing children. The day when she might bear a daughter—for the women of the wood have only daughters—is still many celestial cycles away.

Independence does not always mold itself into beauty, but it does produce strength, intelligence, and a proclivity toward solitude and contemplation. Like mother, like daughter, Nora Lee often thinks and smiles. Only sometimes does the thought bring forth a frown.

First snow lays like white moss; the trim of Nora Lee's great coat brushes it from its newfound bed as she steps carefully through the towering trees until she finds her spot. She stops, looks up.

The sky is milky grey, broken by evergreen branches that make it look like a serpentine river. Snow falls in twirling patterns as if she's looking up the skirts of a hundred bounding dancers.

This is the spot.

Nora Lee slips inside the hollow of one of the ancient hemlocks. She has a view of a small clearing lit by early moonlight. She is prepared to wait and watch the clearing for hours if she must.

Closing her eyes, her frost covered lashes touch her still warm cheek, melting, dripping liquid down her face like slow, silent tears. She doesn't move. She bids her heart to slow, her breath to soften. She smells sap and knows that later when she bathes she will find it forming sticky knots in her hair.

When she opens her eyes again, night has snuck in overhead; stars speckle the winding sky above. The pregnant moon reveals things Nora Lee hadn't seen earlier: an owl's nest high above, perched in the Y of intersecting branches of a tree across the clearing; a burrow beneath a neighbouring tree's roots, either a badger or a fox. And a new addition: a buck, white tailed and ebony eyed, antlers casting shadows that intertwine with the shadows of the canopy as he moves.

Nora Lee loosens the muscles in her left arm; her bow sliding gracefully off her shoulder, down her arm, and into her hand—soundless.

The buck's tail flicks as he kicks at the fluffy snow with one dainty hoof. He bends his neck to nibble at the last of Autumn's greens hidden beneath. Frost from his antlers drips onto the snow, leaving tiny tunnels through the white blanket.

Nora Lee, mere feet away, with ears tuned to the wood's every twitch or turn, can hear the dripping: *Pitter-patter*—like a cloud not committed to pouring, but discontent with passing overhead without making its passage known on the earth below.

Pitter-patter.

Nora Lee nocks an arrow, raises her arm. With a grace born from years of practice she pulls the strong sting back, thumb gracing cheek bone, her gaze locked on the buck.

A white flag. Not a surrender, the creatures of the wood never surrender—a retreat.

Snow flies, the buck bounds away into the trees, leaving fine round hoof prints in his wake.

Something had changed in the wood, the slightest shift that had stopped Nora Lee just before she could loose her arrow. Nora Lee lowers her bow, slowly letting the tension from the string at the same time the pressure and excitement release it's grasp on her heart.

She listens. It was not her that startled the

deer. Something else lurks nearby. The tension, the death grip on her heart begins building again, but it's a different excitement this time.

She gets a chill—a rush over her skin like the fire of a first kiss—and remembers how she used to be afraid of dusk: not of the dark. She knew what was in the dark and that any creature could see her no better than she could it.

But dusk...oh dusk was an old ally of monstrous emanations; fabricated and real. Shadows told wicked stories while early moonlight tempted men down unmarked roads.

Nora Lee allowed herself one breath—the translucent cloud evaporating even as it left her lips.

She was back at the campfire then, that memory of years ago of sitting cross-legged on the cold ground before a dimming fire. Mother had finished braiding her hair. The shadows were growing. The cabin looked warm, inviting, and little Nora Lee longed to be back within it's wooden walls.

But a question lingered in her mind.

Mother was humming and had reached around to hug Nora Lee against her knees.

Dangerous creatures indeed. Her mother's words echoed in her head as Nora Lee stared accusingly at the wood around her—tall trees like skeletal fingers reaching up to grasp the heavens.

The name of this forest is forgotten. Only creatures as old as the forest itself know its name.

Nora Lee tilted back her chin and looked straight up into her mother's eyes—but they were closed. She was singing in a language Nora Lee didn't know.

"Aa aa mažulytę, aa aa gražulytę."

But she did know it. She knew it the same way she knew the way home, or where the deer would be, or when the mushrooms grew. Nora Lee began to hum along, lyrics coming to her head, a memory not quite her own...*aa aa my little girl, aa aa my beautiful little girl...*

"Momma," Nora Lee whispered.

"Mano maža dukteryte..." Mother's song trailed off, caught up in the surrounding web of darkness.

Her mother's eyes opened; a smile pulling the scar on her face taunt. The old wound traced the left side of her cheek bone. A bear perhaps. Or a blade?

"Momma, do you know the name of the wood?"

The man is tall, dark haired and light skinned, though too much time in the glow of last year's Summer has put a layer of freckles on his face and hands. More than one layer: more than one Summer's sun. He's not an old man but old enough to know the wood and its ways.

Nora Lee watches him enter the clearing, taking up nearly the exact same spot where the buck had been a moment before. He carries a bow and a short sword hardly larger than a dagger. Leather gloves hang looped over his belt.

He kneels, pressing a naked palm to the exposed earth and realizes he has just missed his quarry.

Or, maybe not.

He ducks around a tree on the far side of the clearing and returns a heartbeat later with a snare and a struggling grey rabbit. He sets the animal and trap down where the light is best and without hesitation snaps the small creature's delicate neck.

Nora Lee hears the snap; feels the answering chill on her flesh.

There are times when she still hates the

dusk.

When he stands, he is looking directly at her. Their eyes lock like an eclipse, orbs aligned through time and space.

When you meet a creature in the wood... her mother's words vibrate loudly in her mind after years of mental repetition. *Not soldiers...savages.*

The man appears...afraid? Nora Lee cocks her head to the side, aware it is a gesture she's picked up from Pharaoh and yet it comes naturally to her.

The corpse of the rabbit hangs loose in the man's right hand, the trap forgotten in the snow at his boot tips. There is a bird's cry from the sky far above the clearing.

How does one tell the difference between the monsters and the men?

More words come to Nora Lee's mind, but the man finds his voice first.

With a barely audible tremble, he asks: "In which wood do we walk?"

Her mother was rocking her gently against her knees as dusk turned to dark, stars above burning brighter than any lantern made by the hands of men.

Without a word her mother rose and took her hand, leading her back toward the cabin. Warmth waited in there, but it was no longer what Nora Lee wanted: the darkness was still locked to her and she wanted to crack it open, to peer inside.

She stopped, her tiny fingers slipping from her mother's strong ones like sand in an hourglass—and it was as if the wood stopped with her: stopped growing, stopped changing, stopped being.

The wood waited, wanting.

"In which wood do we walk, Momma?" Nora Lee asked again, looking up into her mother's face.

Mother smiled—too wide, teeth too white—and whispered, "You know."

Nora Lee blinked. It was not the answer she'd expected. But it was the truth. She could feel it in her veins, could trace it in the lifelines on her palms.

How does one tell the difference between the monsters and the men?

Around her the air felt changed, renewed with a conscious chill, a knowing breeze.

I've always known, Nora Lee thought, excited.

Her mother was studying her, waiting, Nora Lee realized, on an answer to the very question she had just asked.

In which wood do we walk?

"Death," Nora Lee replied, her voice strengthened by the memory of her ancestors: a matriarch of magic had reigned in the wood since the first sapling took root. "For that is what becomes of any man or beast that should happen upon the monster in the wood."

A phantom weight lowered upon her head; the crown of a genetic monarchy borne in blood rather than in gold or land or title. She had inherited her kingdom in that moment, had learnt its name and its power. Nora Lee could see the smiles of queens beaming down at her, brighter and more numerous than the stars.

A shadow circles in the sky, a small winged silhouette against the backlight of the moon.

Nora Lee had lowered her bow but never taken her arrow from it's spine.

"Death," Nora Lee whispers with the voice

of a million women, and regardless of what tongue the man speaks he will hear her word and know it's meaning. She raises the bow and releases; feathers brush her cheek and sleek carved wood whistles into the night, plunging into the soft warm flesh of it's mark.

The sky cries again and Pharaoh lands on a branch beside Nora Lee.

Her breath surrounds them like a ghostly halo as she reaches out a finger towards him. He raises his head and she scratches him along his throat.

Winter is still young, but Nora Lee feels the wood already slinging off the chill, fighting its way to an early thaw. Perhaps she will have a daughter this summer after all. The wood can be a lonely place, for monsters more than most.

IN THE LAVENDER HAZE

The drag queen plants manicured hands on the sticky tabletop and leans forward, biceps bulging, eyelashes flashing. Cornelius knows his intent before he speaks, the question painted across one cocked brow.

"I ain't love-story material, polar-bear?" The drag queen's voice is deep with a drawl Cornelius can't place.

"Sorry, I'm meeting a friend."

"Do I know her?"

Seeing as she doesn't exist, I doubt it.

He bores of Cornelius's stoicism and leaves, long legs kicking up the hem of a floor length skirt that looks made of bright green paper. Trot, trot, trot, back to the stage he goes, blowing the bartender a kiss before climbing back up to a mic and moving his lips more or less to the fast words and the cacophony of an orchestra that sounds like it's harboring in the apocalypse, again.

Purple liquid swirls in glass mugs, and

girls and boys and things in between all get drunk and howl at the moons.

Polar-bear.

They don't call all cyborgs that, just the rich ones who can afford the white metal from the volcano mines. He ought to be flattered, ought to be proud, or at least pretentious about it, show it off a little—because that's what they expect.

More purple liquid, but he has a metal liver and half a metal brain so only half the headache in the morning when dawn strikes.

Or is it morning now?

Cornelius looks at his wrist—the real one, with purple veins and orange-red freckles—but his watch isn't there.

"O, two-hundred."

The voice takes the seat across the table. Bare chest and black leather pants unbuttoned just enough to show off something red and lacy underneath. A cigarette between two fingers holding it like a tool, not an accessory. His skin is dark like stumbling across a lake at night, impossible to see the bottom.

...two in the morning.

It takes him that long to register the

voice's comment; the hour.

I've had too much...

"Saw you looking for a watch."

"You a dancer?"

A nod. A puff. Lavender smoke. His eyelids are painted gold.

"You're not dancing?" Then: "I'm not looking for a date."

He laughs and it's as dark as his skin. "Relax, polar-bare, I don't want to turn you into a rug—you wouldn't go with the decor in my living room. I just want a beer and a smoke and a break."

They share the silence, passing it back and forth between them. He finds he wants to talk after all.

"You from around here?"

More lavender smoke, this time a ring that halo's his face. "Here? Where's that?"

He shrugs white-metal shoulders. "Point."

A thin wisp of a smile. "Are we playing a game?"

Cornelius stands, wanting out. He isn't looking for a date, just someone to talk to.

Is that why I came in here? To talk?

"Whoa, man, you about toppled right over." And he doesn't sound like a drag queen anymore, just a man helping a drunk find his feet. A long arm wraps around his back. His own metal limb is perched on bare, lean shoulders.

"Come on then. We'll split a cab. And I mean it. Splits. Those sky-divers aren't cheap, and you look like you can afford it."

They make an ungraceful procession toward the door. Cornelius assumes that's the direction they're headed, but he's looking at the floor, at ruby red heels.

"How you walk in those?" He slurs.

"Sober."

Outside the bar they stand together on the grated sky-walk. He feels unsteady and holds onto the building like it's the side of a cliff—and it is. Over a hundred stories down—and they're nowhere near the top.

"Polar-bear." It's not a slight this time and it's not masquerading as endearment either. "I thought you boys were built to hold your liquor."

"Not built. Born," he says, still clinging to the wall, feeling philosophical.

Purple ash turns black and tumbles down to ruby toes and down, down, through the grates.

"We're all built—maybe not of metal though."

"What else?"

Shrug. "Love. Loss. Loneliness, mostly."

He laughs. "How could anyone be lonely in this damn place?" Arms thrown out to encompass the lights, the sound, the human hive buzzing well into the eternal night. "It's the seventh circle."

"You tell me."

There is a click-click as he blinks at the dancer. His one electronic eye capturing every moment, downloading it, processing it, uploading it to sit in a file on a desktop across town, the only source of light in his apartment for his orange kitten to prowl by.

The dancer looks at him. "No one walks into a drag bar like *The Rheingold* in Mid Level on a Tuesday night if they aren't a ferocious shade of lonely."

A sky-diver halts in front of them like it crashed into an invisible wall and they fight a couple women in plaid skirts, too old to actually be prep-school girls, for the back seat.

Victorious and feeling a little better for their small triumph, both ware something the other recognizes as a smile but damned if anyone else would.

"Upper crust, love," he says, sounding like a drag queen again and batting dark eyelashes at the mirror. "77 & Oland."

"Fine, fine—"

The buildings pass in blurs of neon light around them. Cornelius never learned to drive himself, scares the piss out of him. *How do they see? How do they not run into anything?*

"Mostly all automatic now-a-days." The drag Queen's smoking again. "The driver is 'just in case'. We like a man behind the machine. Makes us feel in control."

"You a telepath?" Cornelius asks, registering a chill, his metal body too rigid to indulge it.

Long drag. Puff. The cab fills with a lavender haze. Dark eyes blink again, out the window this time, flirting with the blur of the world outside.

"A little."

They share silence again. No, play tug of war with it.

"You have a cat?"

Nod.

"A real one?"

"You want to see?"

Two parallel vertical lines form right above his nose where his sculpted eyebrows try to kiss each other.

"I really wasn't looking for a date either", says the drag queen.

"Cats make you feel less lonely."

"Who said I was lonely?"

"You did."

"I insinuated —"

"What are you made of then?"

... "Tonight? Starlight and bullshit, I guess. I'd love to see your cat."

"Kitten actually."

"So it is real — driver!"

Eyes and a mustache twitch back and forth in the review.

"Old Town. 82 Pearstall street," Cornelius

mumbles.

A low whistle. More smoke. "You are rich."

"You live ten levels above me."

"Yeah, in a box."

Silence again, shared again.

Should I clear my mind? Do I have anything to hide? No, but I don't like the lookin'.

A sideways glance of suspicion but the dancer doesn't pay him any attention. Puff. Another whistle of awe.

"What? You never seen it before?" he asks, incredulous. You don't work down town and never see the city from a sky-diver.

"Every day of my life. Never seen anything else—ain't that amazing?"

"Maybe. Maybe what else is out there wouldn't amaze you."

A snort. "You sound like you read books."

The mustache speaks. "Pearstall. 82."

They get out separate doors. Slam. Slam. Feet land on grate and ruby heels go tck, tck, tck. The sky-diver is gone. Cornelius feels the tingle on his right bicep, a notification of payment. He brings it up, seeing it in front of his electronic eye while the brown one looks up the synthetic stone steps to the synthetic wood door painted a light shade of indigo.

"Looks like an old movie," the dancer says. "Too bad there's no rain tonight."

"Rain for what?"

"For dancing in." Tck. Tck. Tck.

Three steps and a key in the lock. Metal fingers fumbling.

"How old are you, polar-bear? A key, really?"

He takes the tool and flirts with the lock the same way he seems to flirt with life—and get what he wants. Click.

The lights come on one at a time. Soft yellow.

"That ambiance, though. How much it cost you?"

"Fair amount. The white ones give me a headache."

He laughs, somewhere lighter on the spectrum this time. "Your head must always hurt."

There's a tiny bell running down the hall.

Attached to it are orange ears, a pink nose and gray whiskers.

The dancer stops moving, stops breathing. Face to face with something more graceful and powerful than himself. He drops to his knees and holds out two large, dark hands.

Where'd his cigarette go?

The kitten approaches. She knows she is a lioness. She doesn't bother to smell or lick his offered fingers but bursts forward, head pushing against his flattened palms, tiny voice purring, demanding praise and supplication.

"What's its name?"

"It hasn't got one. Just...Kitten, I guess."

"That's not a name. What about —"

He frowns so deeply the dancer hears it and laughs.

"Oh, come on, I'm not going to give it a stage name. How about..."

Human.

"Human." He picks up the cat and lets it nuzzle against one sharp cheek bone. He winks. "You do read too many books. You're quite the philosopher. Can I feed him?"

"Her."

Two little silver bowls on the kitchen floor. One for food. One for —

"You have milk!" The dancer's voice breaks out of it's drawling resonance.

"Just for the cat."

"If I could afford milk…" He takes off one heel, then the other and drops the rubies to the white artificial tiles. "You know they're giving pets, real ones, to robots over in Draught Point? Says it teaches them how to be more human."

"Should teach humans to be more human."

"That's what the robot pets are for." He stretches, his back arching like Human sometimes does under the heat lamp. The button on his pants is done up now, red lace still peaking above the waist band. "You have a sweater?"

"Why didn't you bring a coat?"

"I was going home, wasn't I? Didn't plan on being hung up at some rich man's place in the Middle level."

"That must happen to you a lot."

The wispy smile returns but then he says:

"I'm just a dancer. Not even that, most nights."

Human bounces ahead of Conelius on the stairs and he takes a gray sweater from the closet. An old sweater but warm and small enough not to hand off the dancer like a sack.

The kitten mews for attention but he sits down at the desktop and plugs in, the tiny needle like connection jutting out from his wrist. Most of the processes are remote but every now and then he has to connect to the mainframe, patch in and do updates. But he stalls them for tonight. He doesn't want to keep his guest waiting.

It's quiet on the stairs. He has a feeling he'll arrive at the bottom and find the dancer has gone. There's some relief in that but disappointment too.

In the kitchen the dancer is still there, shadow like, standing by the back door that should look out on a little back yard but instead has a view of the abyss, the hundreds of stories piled beneath and across from them, the roads, if they could be called that, like canyons stretching down into dark, dark nothingness.

Human is in his arms, purring, rubbing her head against his shoulder.

Slut.

He has a cigarette between his fingers,

unlit.

"You mind?" He asks without turning.

"Ask her."

He looks at the cat then tucks the cigarette behind his left ear. The lobe is pierced with twin gold studs.

He looks back out the glass door, back at the damp, never-waning lights of the city.

Their reflections seem less to stare back at them than through them. The dancer and the cat seemed not to notice.

Cornelius's own reflection is more machine than man. White metal meeting pale, heavily freckled flesh. His orange-blond hair shaved short. Three vertical lines shaved into the side not covered by interlocking metal plates. Both eyes blink, one glowing faintly in the dim kitchen.

His companion is hardly visible in the window. Black pants and black skin. A small silver tattoo of a decorative sugar spoon lays horizontal across an upper rib.

"What's your name?" He hands him the sweater.

The dancer leans forward and lets the cat out of his arms. Four tiny feet pad across the floor to lick at the white liquid in the bowl.

He accepts the sweater and shrugs it on over his head.

"Knight Mare."

Cornelius snorts. "You're real name."

"I lost it."

"How?"

"A chess match. You play?"

"I know how."

The dancer turns and shoves his hands in the front pockets of the sweater as if he might find a tunnel through them to somewhere else.

"You have a home system?"

He nods. "Computer."

The dancer smiles with only half of his lips. "*Computer*? How creative."

"It's simple. And I don't like machines that have names. Chess."

A holographic chess board appears on the island. The dancer goes around the other side and takes up one of the stools, somehow sitting on it like it's a recliner.

"Do you have a name, machine man?" One eyebrow cocked and a hand poised over a white pawn.

"Cornelius."

Pawn to E4.

The hologram glitches, shimmering like tossed confetti as it moves with Knight Mare's fingers. It became solid again upon it's new square.

"What were you before you were a machine, Cornelius?"

Cornelius brings a white meal finger to the board and taps a square, mimicking his opponents move.

Pawn to E5.

A classic opening. A safe game.

"A diver."

Pawn to D3.

"Get blown up down there?"

A blunt question from such graceful lips.

"Yes. That's why I'm rich. That's why I'm broken."

Cornelius frees his Queen.

Knight moves. Another pawn.

Cornelius analyzes the board. His electronic eye scans and compares the moves so far to commonly played openings via a chess database. His real eye blinks at the squares and consults memories stored in flesh.

"You're not playing the game I thought you were," Cornelius says, taking his turn.

The drag queen moves a Knight. Shrugs.

"No one ever is."

The movement of the incorporeal pieces makes the dim light on the countertop sparkle with holographic glitter.

"We're all pretenders. All something of this and three quarters of that. Half robot, half man—half man, half woman." He considers his next move a moment longer, moving further from his planned opening, advancing into enemy territory.

"Not a whole of anything to be found."

Cornelius takes a pawn. Then a Bishop.

Knight kept his Queen defended until the last, until it was too late for Cornelius to see his intention. Then the game was over, and the King laid horizontal on the board, glitching, sparkling.

Calm hangs around Knight's shoulders like a cloak. His teasing grace departed, his easy smile dissipated. His gaze drifts to meet his defeated opponent.

Cornelius can see himself reflected in Knight's dark pupils. He knows, can sense in the man's intense stare, that Knight can see his own reflection too, in the polished surface of Cornelius' metal face.

He blinks, gold eye shadow twinkling like the chess piece. Then he stands and puts his hands back in the pockets of the loaned sweater. He pulls the cigarette from behind his ear and lights it with a lighter from the too-tight pocket of his pants.

"Sorry little lady," he mumbles around the cigarette as Human twines her body between his ankles.

He lets out a long breath of purple smoke. Earlier, Cornelius had thought the lights had turned the colour but there was no such lighting here.

As Knight stands, slouching slightly, bare feet wiggling on the tiles, a shadowed hand running through dark hair, Cornelius can't help but think this isn't the creature he met in the bar.

Cornelius is hesitant to speak, to break the

silence that is already a familiar thing between them, but he can't help himself. He see's something he missed before in this new, strange acquaintance.

"You sound like you read books," he says. "Could you recommend a good one?"

A smile. Dark, charming. The queen slithering back into her crown.

"I've got to be going. Come back to the bar sometime," Knight says.

"Well play again sometime.

"Have we been playing a game?"

He's already halfway to the door. Human sees him out.

Cornelius waves a hand through the chess board and the pieces vanish.

A good way to spend an evening.

Human returns, her hostess duties done, and hops into his lap. He runs a hand along her spine, down her tail, feeling her warmth and the fluttering of her small heart.

Purple smoke still lingered in the kitchen.

Hours pass like this. The sun comes up, unbeknownst to much of the city, much of the world. Somewhere, Knight Mare is sleeping. Somewhere, the multitudes are waking, still enslaved to a glowing ball of light they never see.

Old habits...

Cornelius looks again at his reflection int the window, then the reflection of the reflection in his face and the window and back again.

Just another face in the crowd. Just another face in the crowd.

SPORE562

Intergalactic colonization log. Entry 4,897. Planet: Unknown.

I am alone here.

But I know why I've come. Mother dropped me here. I can't recall her voice—only her last words to me remain, etched into my memory, haunting every thought:

Know this place—let this place know you. Leave a part of yourself behind.

This planet is quiet. I've met no one, nothing, but I feel like I'm beginning to know it.

It's changing seasons, shedding its winter husk for the warming weather. The leaves were blue, but now they're violet and green and alive.

Mother left me with nothing to record my time here, so I talk to myself. I'm a good listener. I think I will remember this place when I'm gone.

The ground is softening. It squishes beneath my feet, but I don't sink: I bounce. I laugh and tell myself how much fun it is. I bounce until the twin moons rise and then I walk again.

I need to know this place, even in the dark.

In the dusk, it is easy to make a misstep, and I tumble into a pool I couldn't see.

I can't swim. I tell myself this again and again.

Icannotswim. Icannontswim. Icannotswim.

My flailing fingers strike something, and I grab on. It's the rocky wall of the pool and somehow I manage to pull myself out, coughing up a sweet liquid thicker than water but not quite honey.

I comfort myself as I sit on the edge of the pool in the twilight. It wasn't as deep as I thought—it rarely is.

"I won't let you down, not ever," myself

tells me.

It's morning and I feel better. I look better too. I can see myself, standing in front of myself. Long limbs, thick, strong chest. Wild eyes, always seeking the horizon. I run my fingers through my hair but Myself does not. I'm relieved that myself isn't a mirror. Though we have so much in common, myself is separate from me.

It is easier to talk this way.

Myself seems to know this place better than I do. We roam, we eat the summer fruit, we bounce on squishy earth, we carve our name in the trees.

I love having myself here. I don't feel so alone.

Something's wrong.

I know because I'm a part of this place

now. Perhaps too much so.

Myself and I stand with our feet in the earth. We are sinking. We are buried up to our calves.

There is something silver on the horizon and it's coming fast.

I remember words of Mother's I'd forgotten:

Leave a part of yourself behind...I will come for you when you have new responsibilities.

I step out of the earth and shake off the numbness of sleep. I had been so comfortable. I hate to leave, but I know I must. I have responsibilities in new places.

I look back at myself and am shocked to see I'm buried up to the waist.

"Come with me," I say. "I need you. I'll drown without you."

Myself opens heavy eyelids and looks up at me. Those eyes are less wild now. I think I see tears in them. I feel tears on my own cheeks.

"You've given me the best of yourself, and I am better for it," I say, my shoulders disappearing into the soft ground. "If it would still your tears then I'd give it all back, but I cannot. You've given me so much that if I returned any of it I wouldn't be myself."

Mother is here. I feel her calling my name. I look back at myself one last time but I am gone, buried in the planet I've come to know better than I knew myself.

But I'm already forgetting.

I walk to meet Mother on unstable feet, over ground and past trees unfamiliar to me. One has my name on it, but I don't recall how it got there.

I am alone here.

I knew all along that one day I'd have to leave. I knew part of me would stay behind, but I didn't know it would be the best part, the part I needed most. The part that kept me afloat.

Mother's ship is cool and safe and fast. I have a bed and food and many things to entertain me but no one to talk to.

My new responsibilities are the same as the last: explore, know the place, leave—leaving a part of you behind. This is how we grow, Mother and I. She says it gives us power and power is safety, that all the places I leave myself are ours. I am a seed, a pollen, a worker bee building a strong intergalactic colony. But it means spreading myself thin, shaving off piece after piece

Mother says I will understand our goal when I see all the beautiful places that will be ours. The next one is bright and covered in clear, shallow oceans. I've already forgotten the last one, but I feel like I forgot something there. Something important.

I've come to know many places and each one has changed me.

Perhaps I have forgotten many things in many places; existential breadcrumbs.

And if I followed the trail backwards what would I find? Would I be waiting there

THEY SAY LOVE IS BLIND

I stare into the top drawer of my dresser, considering the row of blindfolds laid out before me.

"Can I help you, Miss Freeman?" Z asks from its position near the door, voice like static.

Every child receives a robot when they turn ten, to teach them manners and life lessons: nannies that don't need to be paid or fed or have their criminal records checked. Even if you have a stay-at-home parent it's rare to find a home without a robot.

At first, I'd been excited to receive Z, but twelve years without a sliver of privacy had killed the original charm of my metallic companion.

"Yes, Z, tie this for me, please." I pluck a blush blindfold from the drawer and place it into Z's metallic digits. Z has no eyes. The State deemed it far too human a feature. Instead, they have smooth, silver faces that reflect your own in the right light, superimposing your own image onto the metal like a reflection in a hazy pool.

Z places the blindfold over my eyes and ties a bow at the back of my head, fingers clicking softly as they go through the motions. Z takes a couple pins from the dish on my dresser and secures the fabric to my hair to make certain it won't slip. My vision is mostly unaffected, only a little narrowed. I always thought 'blindfold' was the wrong word for something I can plainly see through, but that's what they've always been called. I remember a few years ago there was a push to call them 'Soul Scarfs', but it never caught on.

The State says the eyes expose the essence of a person; windows looking in at the naked soul—which is why they must be covered.

I still recall a hushed conversation overheard on the train on my way to the Academy. I was just a girl then, but it's always stayed with me. One man said to his companion, "They say, if two people stare into each other's eyes for five minutes, they'll fall in love."

He said it like a question but if his friend ever responded I didn't hear it. My mind had already seized on this idea so strongly that I knew it would be one of those things I just never shook free of.

I knew this bit of snatched dialogue between strangers could have been false, a mere hypothetical discussion. After all, I'd heard the stories of girls who'd taken off their blindfolds for a boy, or two.

Did the boys also remove theirs? Did they stare intently into each other's souls? I never asked these questions out loud, but braver girls did. But the answers I sought were silenced by our robots. You didn't speak of such things. Such things didn't *really* happen.

"Are you ready for your date now, Miss Freeman?"

Dating. It's what was expected. *More* than expected. Everyone had three Tickets. Three Tickets for three proposals — or refusals. After you used them all, that was it; single became a life sentence. Singles got no money from the State because they had no children. They had no chance of advancement. If a Single was caught in a love affair that life sentence turned to one of death.

"Yes, Z, I'm ready." Z leaves my room and I can hear it opening the front closet. When I meet Z it's holding a long beige coat by the shoulders, ready for me to slip into it. I'd spent a whole paycheck on that coat. The expense would be worth it — I must look my best tonight. I have a feeling I know what my date has planned. I don't want to give him any reason to get cold feet.

I put the coat on over my black

turtle-neck dress. I do up the big hand-cut wooden buttons and step out of my apartment into the brisk evening air.

"Should I request a cab, Miss Freeman?" Z asks.

I shake my head and start off down the sidewalk, Z's motor quietly revving behind me to keep up.

My heels click on the pavement. I needed the walk. I needed the feeling of blood pumping through my limbs instead of my head.

"The reservation is for six o'clock?" I ask. I already know the answer but anxiety has my mind racing.

Z begins humming behind me. It's communicating with Collin's robot. I know it's searching some type of database, but it's always seemed like a secret club to me—you have to speak a covert language to be allowed in. Sometimes, I hear Z humming from another room in my apartment, or I wake up to the humming even though I've done nothing to prompt Z to search or send information. What do the robots do in the privacy of their electric minds?

I know they relay statistics: sleeping habits, eating habits, what television shows I watch, what I buy, where and when I buy it, and if I ever call the Parents. The State says this information is never held against you.

Robots won't allow you to break the law, and, if you somehow manage to, you're arrested. The robots tell you not to do 'undesirable activities', like cheating on your spouse or watching porn, but because those things aren't illegal, your robot keeps silent about it.

But someone, somewhere knows. That alone keeps most people honest.

"Yes, six o'clock," Z informs me.

I nod, stopping at a light as electric cars and small motor pods whizz in front of me, driving their occupants to their programmed destinations.

A woman stops beside me, pushing a minimalistic stroller—just three thin wheeled legs and a soft cradle-shaped seat with a metal handle, where the woman rests her clean, manicured fingers. Hands that have never changed a diaper—robots do that.

I can see the infant, bundled in a blanket with just its tiny pink head sticking out; eyes uncovered and wide. The State says humans only develop souls after their first year, so there's no point in covering their little lifeless eyes. Still, I look away.

The traffic light turns, and I continue my

walk, distancing myself from the stroller. The streets aren't busy this time of night, but they become more crowded as I leave the quiet, residential area of the city. The streets of the shopping district are still flooded with noise and the skyscrapers that penetrate the clouds are already beginning to pollute the darkening sky with light. This part of the city never day dreamed, let alone slept.

The restaurant is on the thirty-eighth floor of a popular entertainment complex. When I get to the lobby, I stop in front of the glass elevator. It's quarter to six. Collin will be there already. He's always early.

I wait.

At exactly five to six, Z and I step into the glass elevator and start our ascent.

My heart is fluttering in my chest. I take a deep breath in through my nose and close my eyes.

Richard had been the first; a boy I'd met at the Academy, who'd played sports and wanted to travel the world. The Parents made certain I was active, and I took to such a lifestyle naturally. That, and our frequent trips to foreign places, as a result of Fathers work, made Richard interested in me. Every time I met him I played up the traits I knew he admired. I showed him postcards and photos from my travels and invited him on my morning runs. We got on great. He was smitten. After a year of being too close to be just friends, but not quite a couple, he asked me on a proper date. I guess after he got up the nerve to openly express his interest, he couldn't slow himself down because a year later he was on his knee a top a mountain in British Columbia, back dropped by a steamy sunset.

He asked me to marry him. I said no.

One Ticket gone.

"Thirty-Eighth floor," the elevator chimes. Why couldn't robots have voices like that, sweet and harmonic?

The doors open.

The restaurant is decorated meticulously in muted whites and blues. The light fixtures are all the exact same color as the cutlery. When the waiter leads me to our table, Collin's already there.

He's dressed in a finely tailored suit and a pair of grey googles. He has weak vision. The glass in the goggles corrects it, while still hiding the eyes with a thick tinted coating. The goggles have a leather strap keeping them on his head. Apparently, they're fashionable among men now, he would know.

Z and Collin's robot, Y2G—he absolutely

refused to give it a nickname, but at least he doesn't insist on calling it by all twenty-three ID characters—stay at the end of the booth as if standing guard.

"Hello, beautiful." Collin stands, taking my hand in his and kissing the back of it. His palm is warm. Mine is sweating.

"Hello."

He takes my coat and hands it to Y2G.

"This coat is lovely. Is it new?"

I nod. Collin has a taste for extravagance. I wonder how much he's put himself out on the ring. I wonder if he's the type of guy who'd be against re-gifting it.

We sit across from each other and the waiter rattles off the night's menu. I order the chicken, he gets the lobster.

He asks about my work, and I ask about his. Was I still interested in going to meet his Parents next weekend? I had a meeting coming up. Would he still come by and fix the heater in my apartment? My bed was piled high with quilts. Of course, he would take a look at it.

The food comes. We lapse into silence. My chewing becomes a comfortable ambience for my thoughts.

Bruno had been the second. He'd been a chore from the beginning. He liked jazz clubs and writing songs. I'd never particularly been inclined to music or the arts. I knew how to play the piano, not well, but that suited Bruno just fine. He doted on me constantly and tried to help me improve—and I did. I went to all his shows, sipped whiskey with his art friends, and bought him a collection of his favorite records for our third-year anniversary.

He'd proposed drunkenly over a bottle of wine in his chic loft. He hadn't taken the rejection well.

Two Tickets gone.

I spot the waiter coming back to give us the bill. I get a panicked feeling in the pit of my stomach. Is he going to do it? Had I read the signs wrong?

Is he waiting on me?

"Is there anything else we can get for you two?" the waiter asks.

"Actually, yes," Collin said. "A bottle of Champagne, if you will."

I try to hide my relief. I look at him, feigning surprise. "Isn't it getting late for Champagne?"

He smiles. "Darling," he steps from the

booth and stands before me. He gets down on one knee upon the restaurant's blue and white argyle carpet.

My heart is beating so fast it makes me feel like everything else is moving in slow motion.

Collin takes a small box from his pocket. My breath catches. That diamond could cut a girl's eyes just by looking at it.

"Will you marry me?"

He's confident, and calm. I try not to smile, and the effort brings tears to my eyes. Perfect.

"No."

There's a moment of near silence as he stares up at me. All I can hear is the humming noise Z and Y2G simultaneously begin to make beside us. This was Collin's first spent Ticket. My third.

All my Tickets are gone.

The rest happens fast. He stands, baffled. He calmly asks me to repeat myself. I stand too, and, because people are watching, I put my arms around his neck as though I've said yes. There are some hushed sighs and smiles from the nearby tables. To my relief no one makes more of a fuss than that and the restaurant patrons soon return to their meals to give the happy new couple some privacy.

"I know about the men," I whisper. "It's alright, I won't say anything—but we can't go on living a lie."

I'd found out one day, when I'd overheard the tail end of a phone conversation between him and a colleague, which sounded far too personal. After some digging on his home computer, for which Z hadn't even rebuked me, I'd discovered secret relations with at least three men.

Perfect!

I had seriously begun to panic. I'd been young enough when I met Richard that no one had been surprised when I turned him down. The only question when I denied Bruno was why I'd waited so long.

But Collin was a girl's dream come true. What would people think? How would I make them believe there was a good reason for using my final Ticket? Then he'd given me one.

He asks if I'll walk out with him, to avoid a scene. We tell the waiter we changed our minds about the Champagne. We must look like the happily engaged, unable to keep our hands off each other, eager to get home. He pays—he insists—and we get in the elevator with Z and

Y2G, and we remain silent all the way down to the lobby.

"Listen, darling, I'm sorry," Collin says, running his fingers through his hair.

"It's alright." I'm finding it hard to speak. There's a growing tension in my belly and it's crawling up my throat.

"You won't say anything?" he asks.

I shake my head. "But I'll need to tell the Parents. Otherwise, they'll wonder. You understand?"

He nods.

"But they won't say anything," I promise.

"Yes, I know. Thank you." He takes my hand in his again. His palms are sweating now too.

"Thank you, Miss Freeman, for the pleasure of your company this past year. And, I'm sorry again for making you, well—"

"Don't worry about it," I say, wishing he would leave. I shiver at the thought of him saying aloud what I already know to be true.

I'm free.

That thing crawling up my throat is a fit of

uncontrollable laughter. Thankfully, Collin leaves and I rush off to the washroom where I hurry into the stall and lock myself in.

Laughter escapes from me. Great swells of the stuff fill my mouth like cotton balls, making my throat dry and my voice harsh, grating—like Z's. Tears are streaming down my cheeks and for a moment I truly believe I'll never free myself from the grip of this hysteria.

Then, with damp, aching cheeks, I manage to compose myself and leave the confines of the stall. I'm still alone in the bathroom, save for Z.

"Z," I whisper.

"Yes, Miss Freeman?"

"Can you turn around?"

It hesitates. "Turn around, Miss Freeman?"

I know it's silly. The robot doesn't have any eyes to begin with, but it feels right. "Yes, Z. Turn around. Face the door. Tell me if you hear anyone approaching, alright? Can you do that?"

"Yes, Miss Freeman." It hesitates again, making it seem unnaturally human "But, Miss Freeman, I am registering some red flags. You aren't going to harm yourself, are you?"

I laugh. "No, Z. I promise not to harm myself."

The robot's silent. Then, to my great surprise, it turns around to face the washroom door.

Now I'm alone. As alone as anyone could hope to be with a robot. I stand in front of the mirror, looking at myself.

"Should I request a cab, Miss Freeman?"

"Not yet." I stare back at my reflection. I've done it. I've used up all three of my Tickets and no one will be able to accuse me of doing it on purpose. No one would call me an Unloveable, a Loner, a Fallen Woman.

I reach behind my head, carefully removing the pins from my hair. Then I untie the delicate bow Z made and remove my blindfold.

Dark, un-extraordinary brown eyes.

I stare back at them in the mirror. How long do I have before someone comes in to use this washroom? How long can I hide away here, looking into the eyes of my reflection before I must decide what to do with my life?

Five minutes, at least?

SHIPS THAT SINK IN THE NIGHT

Navy blue waves turned to alabaster foam two hundred feet below where Richard kept watch in the old lighthouse. Stan, the elder lighthouse keeper, sat slumped in a chair beside him, untied boots crossed at the ankles and resting on the desk. He slept most of their shifts but he'd wake at the first crackle of the radio.

Richard knew he could rest too if he cared too, but he'd rather look down at the island and the sea that caressed her shores. This day was clear and bright. He could make out all the homes on this side of the island. Each was painted in bright colours to match the paint of their owner's fishing boat–all except one.

The hermit's shack was nestled in a grove of wild rose bushes, hidden both from any wanderers on the road or from children digging for clams on the beach. But nothing was hidden from the watch room.

The shack looked little more than a small brown speck, a tiny stain on the white sand, but Richard remembered how only a night before it had been much less unassuming.

Twilight had just disappeared behind the horizon when Richard had started his solitary walk along the beach that night. A thick fog bank had turned porch lights to fireflies and the ocean into a disembodied roar. Memory alone guided Richard on until suddenly the whole beach was bathed in a brilliant lavender light. Dark waves glowed violet and the sand sparkled like diamonds. In the moment of illumination Richard caught the glint of something small and silver sticking from the sand before the great blinding light retreated.

There could be only one plausible origin for the light–the hermit's shack.

Every hair on Richard's body had stood on end but he'd taken just enough time to reach down through the dark, fingers searching until they touched on something cold and rough. He'd shoved the little unknown treasure in a pocket and hurried on toward home.

"Stan," Richard asked his companion. "Do you really believe the hermit is a...wizard?"

Stan let out a terse guffaw with still shut eyes. "Nothin' but tales made up by silly women to scare the children. Besides, he's more mad scientist than wizard."

"They say his experiments alter time," Richard said. "That people lose hours or days at a time. They say anyone close to the island can be sucked into an alternate timeline where yesterday never happened and today might not matter."

"The stories of silly women," Stan said. "Or worse: sailors."

The static of the radio prevented Richard from pressing the matter. He picked up his pen and log and transcribed the correspondence. He read the letters twice over, not quite trusting his own hand.

"HMS Victory?" Richard asked aloud. "Didn't she go down? Smashed on the ice caps some fortnight ago?"

Stan raised a wooly white brow at him. "No, she's a proud ship, still swimmin'. You must have dreamt it, boy."

"Must have."

Richard's hands strayed absently to his pockets where he was surprised to find his forgotten treasure from the sand. He pulled it out and found a sea battered sugar spoon, unremarkable in every way but for the crudely engraved letters on the handle that read VICTORY.

NOT EXACTLY A COWBOY

Fearghus looked to the North, shielding his eyes from the sun as the sands began to obscure his surroundings, stirring up from the earth in great orange waves. He pulled the black bandanna over his nose and with a nudge from his spurs, urged Thicket away from the patch of dessert thistles she was munching at. Reluctantly, teeth full of the spiny, turquoise flowers, Thicket obeyed and headed East.

Fearghus pushed down the brim of his hat to protect his eyes from the sand.

Crazy Gynts, Fearghus thought. *Even the natives must know the kind of Hell this planet is. Or maybe they smoke too much sand-weed to be bothered.*

There was little civilization here besides the small space port and the cluster of buildings around it that barely passed for a town. It was an irrelevant planet, used infrequently to refuel or grab a beer, if one was truly desperate. The only visitors who stayed more than a few days were Gypsies. Gypsies, and outlaws like Fearghus.

The sands buffeted against Thicket's metallic hide. Her front legs, left shoulder, and most of her face had been replaced with steel and gears. It had been the only way Fearghus had managed to keep her together after the shape he'd found her in. You'd think saving the animal's life and all would make her grateful, but Thicket had the worst temperament of any horse Fearghus had ever met, and he'd met a lot. Met a lot, rode a lot, shot a few, ate one—that had been rough. But, desperate times, and the rest.

The tiny wooden hut looked so out of place next to its neighbor—a large green shipping crate—that Fearghus rubbed his lids to make sure the sand wasn't making him see things. But there they stood, side by side, and atop the shipping crate, a dark figure silhouetted in the sun, blurred by the sand storm.

Fearghus rode Thicket as close as he dared and then pulled on the reins to stop her. She snorted in protest.

"I don't like standing out in this shit any more than you do," Fearghus told her as they waited.

The figure leaped down from the shipping crate. Her dark skin stood out against the bright sand which went completely ignored by her as she strode toward Fearghus and his mount. She wore an ensemble of leather and thin hand-woven cloth that covered only the bare necessities—which apparently didn't include her right breast. She had a sharp, gem tipped spear in one hand, painted and tied with feathers, and a brown leather holster around her hips, complete with a mean looking pistol.

Fearghus had loved that pistol.

Curse this woman.

"Fearghus Fallet." She spat out his name like an insult.

Fearghus pulled his bandanna down around his neck. "Theda," he replied. "I'm in a pinch. Need somewhere to lay low."

Theda narrowed her burnished brown eyes at him.

"Beast," she said, pointing to Thicket with her spear.

"Her name's Thicket."

Theda walked around the horse to get a better look at her metallic muscles. "Why?"

"Because I found her in a thicket."

She grimaced, raising her spear to point at him. "Why metal?"

"She was hurt real bad. Had to patch her up."

"You doctor?"

"No."

She sniffed. A dangerous gesture in all this sand, Fearghus thought.

Theda nodded at him, then started

walking back towards the shipping crate. He'd been accepted, for now, but Fearghus made no move to follow her.

She stopped to throw him a look over her shoulder. "What?"

"Where's your..."

She narrowed her eyes again. Feargus chose his next word carefully.

"Cat." *Demon.*

"Hunting."

Good. Maybe the thing won't be so sour with a full stomach.

Fearghus urged Thicket on after Theda. Inside, the shipping crate had been laid with boards and long green leaves. It wasn't exactly hay, but Thicket didn't seem to mind. She stomped at it with her hoof before deciding it was as good a bed as any.

There was a wooden wall dividing the shipping crate with a small door. Doors were a luxury most native Gynts found extravagant and unnecessary. Fearghus eyed the door and Theda eyed him.

Fearghus looked away first, patting Thicket's nose and ears before standing and leaving the crate—he didn't so much as glance over his shoulder.

I've got enough secrets of my own. She can keep hers.

Theda's hut was hardly home to Fearghus, but there was a strangely familiar mood about the place that grew stronger with every visit. Of course, if he was here, it always meant he was in trouble. Strange, how a hideout was the closest thing he had to roots nowadays.

Gynt huts were triangular, with one point far longer than the others where the sides didn't quite meet. The gap was big enough to walk through but small enough that, with the help of the overhanging leaf roof, it kept out most of the twisting sands.

Theda walked around him and dropped the shutters on the three windows, blocking out the sun and wind.

Fearghus hung his jacket on the back wall where its sagging pockets were least likely to pick up more sand and removed his boots and socks—but kept his gun belt around his waist. Even inside the hut the sand was warm, sticking to his bare toes.

Theda grimaced at his feet as she passed. He didn't blame her. He couldn't remember the last time he'd had a chance to take those boots off.

He threw himself onto one of the rugs in the center of the hut, propped himself up on a rough, thread-bare pillow, and rested his chin on his chest, letting his hat fall over his eyes.

Theda snatched it from his head. "In a pinch?" she said in her thick Gynt accent, waving the hat at him. Gynt was nothing like the Slauzoric languages, but her Vakanish was getting much better. Fearghus often wondered if he was more of a benefit or a detriment to her vocabulary.

"Don't worry 'bout it Theda, I won't bring no trouble here."

She shook her head at him but tossed back his hat. The tangle of wild, dark curls on the left side of her head bounced, while the tightly braided strands on the right swung between her shoulder blades, nearly touching her hips. As she walked away to tend to the small fire pit in the center of the hut, Fearghus tried not to pay too much attention to those hips.

Theda, as he'd found out the hard way, was off limits.

She'd been at the space port's tavern, the day he'd first ended up on Gynt, trying to find someone to buy her goat. Fearghus had readily agreed to purchase the animal and told her he'd pay triple if she threw in some accommodations. If the bounty hunters had managed to tail him to the planet, the last place he'd want to be was in the local watering hole.

She'd agreed, but nearly threw him out
when he'd slaughtered the goat. Gynts were
vegetarians, apparently. He'd tried to explain the
hypocrisy of this, seeing as all her clothing was
made from leather, but she'd known almost no
Vakanish at the time and had instead gotten her
point across with a few solid whacks to his head
with her spear.

He'd learned a lot more about Gynt
culture since then, like the fact that Gynt women
took their virginity far more seriously than
Vakanish women. She'd worn basically no
clothes all day, then had given him a significant
look of satisfaction when he'd removed his
shirt—how was he to know that was a
customary Gynt gesture, to show the host or
hostess that you accepted and appreciated their
hospitality? Where he came from girls didn't
just invite any bloke back to their home if they
didn't have a mind to have their way with him,
even if said bloke had bought their damned
goat.

He'd left the sandy carpet she'd specifically
laid out for him—which, he admitted in
retrospect, was a pretty solid hint she had no
intention of sleeping with him—and sauntered
over to her bed. She'd been sleeping soundly,
her curly hair spilling over the mattress, not a
single thing on her person in way of clothing.
He'd brushed her ankle, gently, to wake her, and
before he knew what was what he was on his ass
in the sand with a lump on his head you could

see from space. Theda had let loose a slew of Gynt curses which Fearghus didn't need a dictionary to understand. He'd spent the remainder of the night under the stars, alone, with sand in unmentionable places.

The next morning, he'd appropriated a book on Gynt history and culture from the nearby town, and returned to Theda's hut with a lei of thistles and a hare's foot (the traditional Gynt gift of apology), as well as a can of Vakanish chocolates (the traditional "I was a dink" gift of males everywhere).

Flowers, chocolates, a dead animal's foot — a down right gentleman, I was.

A curious humming sound outside pulled Fearghus from his musings. Theda jumped to the window and peeked under the shutter. Her hand had instinctively gone to her gun when she'd heard the noise.

Good girl.

Fearghus eyed his own gun, still too new and shiny for his liking. It was easily inferior to the one he'd lost to Theda in that bad bet.

Theda took a green scarf from a hook by the entryway and wrapped it around her head, mouth, and nose. If she was covering up, then a serious storm was blowing in.

Great, I'm being hunted and there's a hell-storm brewing. Can this get any better?

"What was that sound?" Fearghus asked. It had sounded like a motor perhaps. "That hum?"

"Out window," she said.

"What's out there?"

"Out," she gestured towards the window with her spear. "Door."

"Door? I thought you wanted me to go out the window?"

She gestured at the window again. "Out. Hide in door."

The door in the shipping crate.

Fearghus grabbed his boots and jacket and climbed out the back window as Theda left through the front of the hut.

The wind was vicious. Fearghus tied the strings of his hat tight under his chin so he wouldn't lose it. As he pulled on his boots, he heard a soft growl at his back. Slowly, he turned around, hands up, to face a large Gynt leopard.

Its body was an orange-beige colour, only a shade or two lighter than the sands. Its pointed ears stood up around tufts of teal fur, and more patches were stuck between the pads of its toes and dotting its hindquarters and tail.

Luckily for Fearghus, only the female leopards had the long, saber-like front teeth that the species was known for. This one, in comparison, was mildly less intimidating.

"Hello, Serge," Fearghus said. It earned him another growl and a pair of hunched shoulders.

"Listen, your mommy said it was okay that I'm here. She might be in trouble though. Go out front there and protect her, 'ight?"

Curse this cat.

Serge let out another deep growl, and his tail flicked—but something, inaudible to Fearghus, caught his interest out-front and he went bounding around the corner of the hut.

Fearghus let out his breath and peeked around the other corner of the hut. Two sand buggies were parked some ways off. It was their motors that Fearghus and Theda had heard. The owners of the buggies were meeting Theda in front of the hut.

There was a man wearing the uniform of the International Border Police, and a woman in a different, navy uniform. He knew that woman, even with the scarf covering most of her face.

Shit. How did she find me this time?

They were too far away for Fearghus to hear their conversation, but he watched as Theda circled them as she had done to him and Thicket. While she had their attention, Fearghus made a run for the shipping crate. He barreled through the open doors and tumbled in beside Thicket. Thicket made to get up at her master's sudden arrival, but Fearghus quickly soothed her, petting her mane and whispering to keep her calm. The horse snorted, but settled down again.

Fearghus went to the door in the wooden wall of the crate. It was locked. He rolled his eyes and waited, listening until a particularly loud gust of wind blew by the open crate doors and then he kicked in the door.

He hurried inside and shut the door as best as the busted latch let him. The room was dark, but the wall didn't go all the way to the top of the crate so there was just enough light for Fearghus to notice (and not trip over) the cloth bags on the floor at his feet.

He opened one, and grabbed a handful of little brown pellets. He brought them to his nose; they smelled like dirt, and fish. Chicken, maybe.

Cat food?

Fearghus dropped the pellets and brushed his hands together. There must have been thirty bags of the stuff in the little room. The only other object was a long chest which he was relieved to find unlocked. He opened it and found yet another bag. He moved to pick it up to move it out of his way, but struggled to budge the bag. It was astonishingly heavier than a bag of cat chow.

His jaw dropped when he untied the bag and looked down. In it sparkled dozens, maybe even hundreds, of polished green gemstones.

Where did Theda get this loot?

No time for that now. He shoved the bag as best he could to the far side of the chest and squeezed in beside it. He knew the chances of someone not looking for him in there were slim—it was a horribly obvious hiding place—but he hoped, for that reason, that his pursuers wouldn't bother to look.

Surely, she knows I'm more competent than this. Right?

Even if she didn't, he would be ready and waiting for her to open the lid.

Fearghus removed the gun from his hip holster and made sure it was loaded before closing the lid of the chest. Then thought struck him.

My gun! Theda's got my old gun!

There was no way Janelle wouldn't recognize his favorite pistol.

Fearghus busted from the crate and tore out of the room, slapping Thicket on the rear as he ran past.

"Come on girl, I may need ya!" He ran out

into the swirling sandstorm, Thicket close behind. Seeing through the billowing gusts of sand was near impossible, but a muffled gunshot gave him a fair idea of where the excitement was.

Fearghus quickly pulled his bandana over his face again, regretfully relinquished his hat to the sands, and tied back his shoulder length, brown hair where it wouldn't fall into his face while he battled his pursuers and the elements.

He grabbed Thicket's reins and hauled himself into her saddle. She didn't mind the sand, but he worried briefly how it was affecting her gears before kicking her into a gallop. They rode off in the direction of the shot.

The storm raged on and Fearghus strained to hear something human. Finally he caught sight of a tall figure silhouetted behind a wall of blowing sand. He pulled hard on the reins and took aim.

Sighing, he lowered his gun again. It was impossible to tell who was who in this storm—he couldn't risk a shot and hit Theda by mistake.

And would I really be alright plugging Janelle full o' lead?

He was glad he didn't have time to ponder that question. He swung a leg over Thicket's back and jumped to the ground. Then, with a running start, he leaped for the figure's knees, taking him out and sending them both tumbling over each other in the sand.

A very surprised Border officer rolled over. He coughed as he tried to simultaneously scramble backwards and grab for his gun.

Fearghus punched him in the side of the head, knocking him backwards before grabbing a fist-full of the officer's jacket and punching him in the teeth.

He left the unconscious man in the sand and raised his gun before heading towards another dark, writhing shape in the storm. As he got closer, gun at the ready, he recognized the two women: Janelle, with her hands around Theda's throat and Theda, repeatedly slamming her knee into Janelle's abdomen.

Fearghus had fantasized about women fighting over him before, but he had envisioned slightly different circumstances, with a lot less sand and less clothing.

The roar from behind gave him barely enough time to roll out of the way as Serge went soaring over his head. The Gynt leopard pounced on Janelle. She'd lost her scarf in the struggle, and Fearghus could just make her out, pinned underneath the big cat.

What took him so long? Fearghus thought, glad to see the animal for once.

Then there was red on the sand. And screams mixed with the howling winds.

"Call him off!" Fearghus shouted to Theda.

Theda was digging her pistol out of a dune. "She tried to kill me!"

"She's my wife!"

Theda raised her eyebrows at him, and though only half her face was visible, Fearghus could tell she thought he'd just said the stupidest thing she'd ever heard.

"Serge!" she called, whistling sharply. The leopard came bounding over to her.

Fearghus walked over to Janelle. She was on all fours, struggling to get to her feet. Her short black hair stuck to her forehead with sweat, and her eyes had dark rings of exhaustion beneath them. Her shirt was torn and bloody.

"Fearghus," she said, in a weak, barely audible voice. She looked worse than he'd ever seen her. She reached a trembling hand up for help.

Fearghus holstered his gun and gave her head a hearty kick with his boot.

There was a honky-tonk song playing on the buggy radio. Theda taped the dash in rhythm with the twangy voice. Janelle, unconscious and gagged with one of Theda's scarfs, sat slumped in the back seat between a bag of precious gems and a bag of smelly cat food.

Serge had crammed himself in the trunk, unwilling to be left behind, and rested his chin lazily on the headrest in front of him. Blueish drool was slowly running from his jowls onto the seat cushions.

Fearghus buried his face in his hands.

"Ship?" Theda asked, turning the music down. They were waiting for the winds to lessen. The tight town streets acted like wind tunnels, making walking even five feet between buildings a struggle for survival. The buggy shook, but had been built heavy to stay grounded, in worse weather than this.

"Yes, I'll get us a ship," Fearghus said. "I need a few things first."

He leaned forward, trying to judge the weather beyond the wind-shield. Things seemed to be dying down. He opened his car door. "Stay here."

Slamming it behind him he made for the nearest store.

A sleepy cashier perked up as he came in. He said something in Gynt, then must have noticed Fearghus' light tan and excessive layers of clothing, because he immediately repeated himself in broken Vakanish.

"You out in storm?"

Fearghus discreetly grabbed a box of candied almonds from a shelf while looking around the store.

"It's not so bad now." Pretending not to find anything of interest, he wandered up to the till. "I need a pack of your finest."

It took the man a moment to realize he meant the cigars behind him. "Oh yes, these, sir."

He took down a small yellow box and laid it on the counter. Fearghus flipped it over to look at the price. He rolled his eyes. Anything sold on a space port was jacked up to highway robbery.

He bought them anyway, pocketed the candy as compensation, and headed back to the car.

He found Janelle awake and glaring in the back seat, scarf still in her mouth. He threw the candy and cigars on the dash and put the key in the ignition.

"Are we ready to go?"

Theda was sitting stone still, looking at

him like he might spontaneously combust.

He sighed. "What?"

She thought about it for a moment. "Why cigar?"

"To bribe the guard at the gate."

She paused again. "Candy?"

Fearghus ground his teeth. "I'm munchy."

Theda crossed her arms.

Fearghus sighed. "You took off her gag, didn't you?"

"She say you stole her daughter — "

"*Our* daughter."

"And lied about being pilot — "

"I am a pilot."

"And she say that — "

"Yes, I'm a horrible husband! I thought I wanted to settle down, thought a wife and a home and a family would make me a respectable man. Well, it didn't. So I left."

He jabbed an accusing finger at Janelle, still glaring and breathing heavily through her gag.

"Whatever lies she told you, I am a good

father! I see Tahra as much as I can, and I give her everything she wants. Never missed a birthday in all six years, never! And this damned woman would turn her into a tool, a drone for that corrupt government she worships!"

Theda laid a hand on his shoulder. Fearghus was gripping the steering wheel with both hands, turning his knuckles white.

"I won't let her do it," he said softly.

He closed his eyes and took a few deep breaths. Then he turned to Theda, and for the first time in a long time, he begged.

"Theda, I can't give up my little girl. That woman'll turn her into a government robot, send her off to some mind-wash academy where they'll cut-and-paste some cookie-cutter Girl Guide personality on her so she can be screened and sorted into a cubicle somewhere on the far side of the Galaxy. I want her to be free, to choose her own fate, like you. Do you understand?"

She smiled wryly. "I do no academy."

Fearghus laughed, and let the tension leave him. "No, but you don't need it. You're your own kind of brilliant, Theda."

She grinned. "I help."

"Good."

"And you help me."

Fearghus threw her a curious glance. "The gems?"

"I sell, and buy ship."

"What?" Fearghus bet those gems would buy far more than a ship. It was likely Theda didn't even know what they were worth. "You want a ship. Theda, you can't even fly."

"You pilot. Can't be hard."

He rolled his eyes. "Alright. I know a guy who can sell them. He'll take a cut, but he owes me one so it shouldn't be too steep."

"You owe me one."

"I'll owe you much more than that, if we manage to get off this planet alive."

"Good. Now what?"

He opened his door again. "I need a drink."

Theda's eyes widened as he headed towards the tavern. She hopped out her side of the buggy.

"What about wife?"

"Come on, she's not going anywhere. Serge will keep an eye on her."

Reluctantly, Theda followed him.

At this time of day, and at the tail end of a sand storm, the tavern was nearly deserted. Fearghus walked straight to the bar.

"I want to buy a case of your finest malt," he said to the bartender.

The tall Gynt man eyed him. "You paying cash?" he said in a perfect Vakanish accent.

"It's prepaid."

The bartender nodded and walked around the bar and out through a back door. He came back shortly carrying a large crate about four feet long with a whiskey label burned into the wood.

"Fragile," the bar tender said, sliding it onto the bar.

Fearghus nodded and leaned across the bar. "There's a shipping crate a few miles west o' here," he said, voice low. "Inside is a horse. I need you to send someone, preferably someone who's real good with mean animals, to pick her up and ship her to me."

He took a napkin and wrote an address on it.

"Ship it here. Can you do that?"

The bartender took the napkin and nodded. "I know a guy."

"Perfect." Fearghus grabbed one handle of

the wooden crate. "You heard the man, Theda, this is very fragile."

She rolled her eyes and took the other handle. They carefully slid the crate off the bar and walked it back out to the buggy.

"I know a guy," Theda repeated.

"It means, 'I can handle it, but it's best you don't know the specifics.'"

Theda sniffed. "Cowboy."

"I'm not a cowboy."

"Outlaw."

"I'm — " They put the crate down in the sand. "Alright, I am that."

Fearghus unloaded Janelle, throwing her over his shoulder. He hurried off to the alleyway beside the store and leaned her against the wall.

He sighed and wiped his forehead with the back of his hand. "Nothin' personal, I just think you're a bad mother, is all. And your new husband's a goof. He's got no business around my Tahra."

Janelle kicked out ineffectively at him and spat some words he was glad to have muffle by her gag.

"Oh, c'mon. Someone'll find you before the next sand storm blows in." *Probably.*

Fearghus, satisfied and having nothing else to say to her, headed back to the buggy. Theda had moved the bag of gems onto the floor so that the crate fit in the back seat. With everything taken care of, they climbed in and headed for Port.

The Gynt Space Port was small, surrounded by a tall wire fence that Fearghus knew gave you a good jolt if you tried climbing it. Most of the pads were empty, but Fearghus could see a few ships docked down the far end.

Fearghus drove up to the gates, and a man wearing what looked like a bee-keepers hood, stepped up to the car.

"They make you stand out here in the storms?" Fearghus asked as the man approached his window.

"There's a little nook we hole up in, but if anyone official comes by we have to be ready to take their identification and let them through," the guard said.

"Does that happen often?"

"Uh, does what happen?"

"Do official or important people come by here? It's such a small port, after all."

The guard puffed up his chest. "Just this morning we had a woman come through. A detective-type if you ask me."

Fearghus laughed. "Who? Janelle?"

"That was her name!"

"She's just a bounty hunter, we both are. You see, she's my partner." Fearghus looked over his shoulder dramatically at Theda before leaning towards the window. "You know, I'm not supposed to say anything, but this here is our catch. Blood-thirsty criminal, she is. I've been here undercover for months."

Theda snorted and mumbled something in Gynt, which luckily, the guard didn't seem to speak. His eyes nearly glazed over as he leaned closer to the window. "Did she kill somebody?"

"Somebody? You don't even know the half of it." Fearghus grabbed the box of cigars off the dash and patted his jacket pockets. "Say, you got a torch?"

The guard nodded vigorously and brought a lighter out of his pocket.

"Thanks." Fearghus took it and made to light a cigar, then stopped. "Say, I told Janelle I'd get our chopper started up. Think you could point me in the right direction?"

"Sure thing, I just need some identification."

"Now, I don't have none, you know, being undercover and all," He waved the cigar around as he spoke. "You think you might be able to just let me through? I really need to get her locked up before the sedative wears off."

"She's sedated?"

"Oh yeah. She's so vicious though it don't put her right out, just makes her drowsy. You know?"

"Sure, sure."

"So, about that chopper?"

"I guess it wouldn't hurt — "

"Great! Here, take the rest of these for your trouble." Fearghus threw the pack of cigars at him. "Do me a favor, when Jan comes by, don't tell her I had them on me. I told her I quit."

"Wow, sure thing! Thanks!"

The guard walked back to the gates. Soon, they rolled open for the buggy to drive through.

"It's pad twelve, out by the main dock," the guard called as they drove past.

"Blood-thirsty?" Theda said, arms crossed.

"It's all about telling a good story. Not that it was hard. That man must have the most boring job in the galaxy. I didn't even have to bribe him."

"She really bounty hunter?"

Fearghus nodded. "She used to be. When she was fun."

Fearghus drove the buggy along the thin road until he found the ship, and parked right under the wing. "Alright, we need to get everyone and everything on board as quickly as possible."

Theda got out, carrying a bag of cat food, Serge following right behind.

I can't believe I let myself get talked into bringing that over-sized cat.

Fearghus took a deep breath and managed to heave the bag of gems over his shoulder. Once the bags were inside he and Theda brought in the crate. He placed it down gently, right behind the pilot's seat.

"Teach," Theda said, sitting down in the seat beside him.

"Ground rules: no lessons if we are escaping from a hostile environment. Yes, that includes right now. And you wear normal clothes when we're in public places. Other planets are not quite as free-spirited as Gynt. Got it?"

"I wear my clothes on ship?"

Fearghus shrugged. "You won't find me complaining."

She nodded, seeming satisfied.

Fearghus got the engine running and tore out the tracking system installed in all Government ships. Doing so was supposed to make the ship inoperable, but he'd learned ways to get around that years ago.

With everything ready for take-off, he got up from his seat and knelt beside the crate. Using the handle of his knife, he carefully pried open the lid.

Inside was a little girl, sleeping soundly, a small plastic oval in her mouth keeping her vitals up. Her cheeks were rosy red and big, puckered on each side with dimples even in sleep. She had her mother's black hair, and Fearghus' tan skin.

"She want to come with you?" Theda asked.

Fearghus gathered his daughter in his arms, careful not to wake her. "Yes. She wants to be a pilot."

Theda thought about that for a moment. "She wakes and says she like cookie-cutter cubicle, I kill you and take her back to wife."

Fearghus laughed quietly. "Fair enough."

He carried Tahra through the ship to one of the two small rooms on board. Theda had already put her things in the other, and Serge had made himself comfortable on her bunk. That was fine with Fearghus. They had a long couple days of flying ahead with where he planned to go, so the only sleep he would be getting were naps, and only once he showed Theda enough for her to mind things in his absence.

He laid Tahra on the small bunk and rested her head on the pillow, taking the plastic oval from between her lips. He pulled the box of candy from his pocket and laid it on the bed beside her. "Here you go, Munchkin, we're going on an adventure, just like Daddy promised."

He returned to the cockpit and shooed Theda away from the many blinking screens and buttons she was inspecting. When Fearghus took the ship out of Gynt's atmosphere, she was nearly standing on her seat, clinging to the chair like she was the sole force keeping herself in the ship.

Eventually, once he was sure they weren't being followed, he pointed out some of the basic functions of the ship. He also gave her a Vakanish dictionary to read, which he'd found by the toilet.

With a wider vocabulary—and a proper shirt—he imagined she'd get on just fine, in most space ports at least. He surprised himself by being grateful to have her along. She wouldn't have been his first pick for a substitute mother, but an extra pair of hands, particularly feminine ones, would go a long way in taking care of Tahra.

"We go sell sparkles now?" Theda asked.

"The gems?" Fearghus asked. "Not yet. First we have to find a place to lay low."

Theda cocked her head. "We in a pinch?"

"Just a little one."

"Where we go now?" she asked.

Fearghus smiled. "I know a guy."

A PUNISHMENT FOR FUTURE WRONGS

"When are you from?"

"Relatively soon," the man replied.

Natasha had been washing her hands in the sink. She'd cut up a bowl of strawberries for Molly to take outside with her while she played in the backyard. She'd bought this house for the yard, and the swing set out back which came with the property.

When she'd turned around, drying her still pink hands with a towel, he'd been sitting there at the kitchen table.

She demanded how he'd gotten in and he told her that he'd traveled—from the future—directly into her kitchen.

"Why are you here?" she asked, after she'd locked the back door, hoping Molly wouldn't decide to come in any time soon. Natasha wondered if she ought to call the police. The man was obviously deluded.

Though he didn't look particularly dangerous. He pushed his glasses up on his thin nose. They had no frames, only glass and wiry arms, and the lenses seemed to swim with transparent colours, like the liquid Molly used to blow bubbles.

"It's about your daughter, I'm afraid," the man said.

Natasha shivered from the stranger's mention of Molly. She resisted looking out the window at the swing set. "What about my daughter?"

"Mrs. Nichols, I am here to sentence you for a crime you committed."

"What crime?"

"That's classified."

"When did I commit it?"

"That's also classified."

He removed a glossy silver badge from his jacket and laid it on the table between them. "This is my certification, and this — " he handed her a large rectangular device that looked like a smartphone, but not any she was familiar with. "Is my certificate of time travel and my 'Order to Sentence' papers. The latter outlines your sentence and your choice of punishment."

"My choice?" Natasha said, putting down the dish cloth and scrolling through the documents on the phone. They looked legitimate, but she wasn't sure how one would know the difference.

"Oh yes, the future is very accommodating! We make sure everyone has at least two options when it comes to their own sentencing. It makes them feel more engaged with the process, which we find beneficial to the rehabilitation of the incarcerated."

"So—in the future—I'm in jail?"

"Oh no, Mrs. Nichols, the choice you made lets you avoid incarceration."

"What's my punishment then?" Natasha said, finding it hard to believe she'd ever commit a crime. "What does it have to do with Molly?"

"You have chosen to never have had a daughter."

Natasha gasped. "I would never choose such a thing!"

"Oh, but you do—you will." The man scrolled down to the last document and there, at the bottom, was Natasha's very own signature.

"How did you get this?" Natasha demanded. Her hands were beginning to tremble violently as she grasped the device, staring down at the scrawled initials she knew to be hers.

"You wrote it of your own accord, Mrs.

Nichols."

"I did not! I have never seen these documents in my life."

"Yes you have. In your future."

Natasha handed the device back to the man. "I'm going to have to ask you to leave now."

"Of course, Mrs. Nichols." The man stood. "I am required to inform you that these sentences can be unsettling. However, we have mastered our executions so they are expedient and as painless as possible. There will be a lasting sense of loss, of course, but you'll never remember what it is you're without."

He hesitated, then: "We try very hard to make the transition as smooth as possible, but sometimes things are missed. Nothing's perfect, you understand."

Natasha stared at the man as he went to the door. She knew the man must be crazy, but she asked the question she'd be harboring anyway. "When will my sentence be carried out?"

"It is already done," he said. "I'm just a bureaucrat, Mrs. Nichols, my partner is the executioner. I'm afraid I don't have the stomach for such things."

He nodded and the lenses of his glasses

turned black. He was taking something from his pocket when she shut the door on him.

Natasha locked the door and the deadbolt.

Unnerving man, she thought, her back pressed to the door. Should she still call the police?

She took a deep breath and tried not to rush back to the kitchen. She felt silly. Molly was fine.

Natasha opened the back door and called into the yard.

"Molly."

There was no response.

"Molly!"

Natasha heard the front door open. Fearing the stranger had returned, she grabbed a broom from the hall closet and went charging into the front room.

"Darling?" Her husband stood, briefcase in hand, looking quite confused about his wife's erratic entrance. "What on Earth are you doing?"

"They took her, George."

"Took who?"

"The girl."

"What girl?"

Natasha lowered the broom. What was her name? Hadn't she just said it?

"She was mine," Natasha said, confused, relinquishing the broom to her husband. There was a hollowness forming in her chest.

George smiled. "You mean Molly? You don't have to be sad about that! I've got a surprise for you. Wait here."

Mr. Nichols put down the briefcase and broom and went back out the front door. Natasha was relieved. Her husband must have brought back her little girl.

George returned carrying a small, golden, floppy eared puppy.

"Let's meet your new mom!" George said, handing the animal to his wife.

Natasha, surprised, held the animal at arm's length. The hollow feeling continued to grow.

"I know it's not Molly, but she was an old dog. She's in a better place now," George said, anxiously watching his wife. "Now you have a new puppy to love."

Natasha pulled the puppy to her chest. Stroking its soft blond fur, she forced a smile.

George relaxed, relieved. "I'm glad you

like her. We bought this old house for the yard, so Molly would have room to run around. It would be a shame to have it go to waste now—and after having that old play set dug up, too.

The cavity had stopped expanding. The cold dark walls had solidified into something sad and bottomless, but static.

Natasha went to the kitchen with the puppy in her arms, and looked out the window at her empty backyard.

The puppy began to lick her fingers with its slimy tongue. Natasha noticed her fingertips were stained slightly pink.

Nothing's perfect.

"Well, what will you call her?" George asked.

"Criminal," Natasha said, hugging the small animal. "Because she stole my heart."

STRANGE FOLK

The Traveler stood in the middle of the road with the hem of his pant legs becoming damp in the puddles, and the blurry glare of the street lights reflecting off the wet pavement. He wasn't a very tall man and he wore a pageboy hat and carried a briefcase. The briefcase, like his heart, was empty.

A cab pulled up in front of him and stopped.

"You Ned?"

He was not, but he nodded and got in the backseat with his briefcase.

The cab pulled away before asking where the traveler was going. That wasn't unusual, there was really only one direction to go down this road and they had a ways to go before decisions had to be made regarding specific destinations. But, this wasn't at all where the Traveler desired to go.

"The other way," the Traveler said.

The cab driver adjusted the mirror and looked back at him, the reflection of two grey eyes as watery as the rain wet street. He didn't believe him.

The Traveler took off his glasses—which he hadn't been wearing before, but the driver didn't seem to notice—and wiped them on his shirt, making the glass sparkle.

A huff from the driver had the cab pulling a u-turn. The car's headlights shawn on the row of middle class turned lower class homes—porches with old lawn chairs, or couches that didn't belong outdoors, three year old Christmas lights dimmed to pastels, and half neglected flower pots turned ash trays—until the vehicle was pointed in the right direction.

"Just the ocean this way," the driver said.

The Traveler put the glasses on his face.

"And you don't want to be down by the ocean this late, on a night like this."

That interested the Traveler. For what kind of night was this? He met the driver's gaze in the rearview. "Is it supposed to storm tonight?"

The driver's eyebrows came together in a wrinkle. Thick eyebrows, dark skin. His flesh said he was from away but his accent admitted he'd lived here his whole life. "No storm, but the rocks are slippery when it's like this, dewy like. We lose a bunch of your folk every year."

The Traveler smiled. "My folk?"

"Tourists."

The Traveler laughed. "I'm not really a tourist." He looked out the window, watched the row of houses dwindling until it was small shack after small shack, each separated by half a mile of rock and rough brush. "Well, I'm something like a tourist."

The road became less pavement and more dirt. The Traveler loved it; the hollow hole in his chest longed to be far from the metaphorical "beaten path".

Driving at night had become a chore for the traveler, his eyes getting weary, which is why he hired cabs now. But he still liked to feel the wheel beneath his hands from time to time. Especially in places like this; roads that went nowhere.

"But all roads lead to Rome," he mumbled to himself as he adjusted the rearview mirror. He looked at his reflection and found the hat no longer fit quite right so he removed it and laid it on the passenger seat on top of his now full suitcase.

The tires hummed against winding road as it snaked around the dark coast line, the black Atlantic rocking to his left. The Traveler rolled down the windows with a click of a button on the door. Salt air swept in, coating the back of his throat with the taste of the sea as he laughed.

Land fell away as he approached a bridge built of massive rocks, a sea wall that stretched from the mainland to the small island which supported a lighthouse. On stormy nights waves crashed against the wall, flooding the bridge, but tonight was fairly calm for those familiar with the usual push and pull of the sea.

The cab rolled across the bridge. The Traveler basked in the temporary darkness at its center, too far from the lights on either side. Blind but for the lights on the dash, the smell of brine in his nose, and the roaring of the waves in the night.

The vehicle stopped, parked by an oversized lawn chair, a novelty tourists liked to take photos on. This place seemed like the end of the world but people flocked here every year to glimpse it's shores. The water was not crystalline blue, it was cold enough to stop your heart, and fishing boats out numbered yachts 100 to 1. And still the people came. What did they come for? The Traveler didn't know. He wasn't that kind of traveler, but he knew what he had come for.

Stepping out of the cab the Traveler looked around the dark shore. Her hair graced her shoulders now. Long thin legs as graceful as a dancer's walked around the cab. Stretching aching limbs, tired of cramped quarters.

She took the suitcase and the hat from the passenger seat and left the empty cab to wander around the parking lot. Searching.

The wind picked up from time to time. Nothing ferocious, just an echo of the gales it was capable of crafting.

The Traveler's search was not long. She picked up a discarded beer bottle from the dirt. It wasn't very old but the salt air and rain had had it's way with it. The logo tore away easily, damp, tattered paper the Traveler let the wind take.

Hat and bottle in one hand, heavy suitcase in the other, the Traveler kicked off her shoes and started for the rocks. They were slippery, as the cab driver had warned; it was easy to see how foolhardy tourists could fall in.

The Traveler found a stable seat on the flat top of one of the rocks and laid the suitcase beside her. The leather was a worn tan, bleached from many days in the sun. The Traveler set the bottle between her knees and rolled up the pageboy hat as tight as she could and stuffed it into the bottle. You would be surprised how much one could fit into a bottle. Some things get caught at the neck but with a little maneuvering of the fingers, the Traveler could get anything to fit. A handful of sand followed the hat, scooped up from between the rocks, wet and clumped with seaweed. Then the glasses, too big for her face now and sliding slowly down her nose. She removed them and folded down the arms. They too found their way inside the maroon glass.

The Traveler could feel the surf sprinkling her skin, cold drops like ice that stung and made her feel a little less hollow. She held the mouth of the bottle out toward the Atlantic to collect a smattering of the vast ocean.

Then she opened the suitcase. Inside was the finale stuff to fill her bottle. Clay like, she had to mold it in both hands, shaping the soft parts into ribbons that would fall easily into the bottle. This was that something special she always searched for to add to her bottles, the post cards she sent home. Sea and sand, earth and branch, though stamped with the unique fingerprints of its geography, could be collected from anywhere. People though, people were different. Place shaped them into things no one could perfectly replicate.

Not even the Traveler.

She pulled on the thin chain around her neck, tugging the cork on the end of it out from under the flannel button up shirt. She took it off it's chain and plugged up the bottle with it, hammering it against the rock for good measure. Inside the contents spun and mixed, like folding sugar into butter. They were teal and deep gray and gold and sparkled with the intensity of a tiny galaxy.

The wind whistled again as she stood,

locks of auburn hair tousled and wet, just beginning to knot. The Traveler started to hum a shanty she'd learned not long before, something old but still sung to young ones in place of lullabies. Then she faced the waves and tossed the bottle into the sea.

She closed and collected her suitcase, and took another moment to appreciate the dark swell and ebb of the water. One thing the Traveler liked about the Atlantic was that you could never catch your reflection in it.

Time to go, she turned from the ocean and made her way back over the rocks. She left the cab, opting to walk back over the bridge and along the shoulder of the winding road. It would give her time to decide who and where she would be next. That was the freedom of being a Traveler, you could be anyone you liked, and all you had to do was leave your heart at home.

GODBOT

Melody flexed, muscles straining against the restraints that kept her body from responding physically to the images of the nuclear wasteland presented in panoramic VR behind her goggles.

Not VR, she reminded herself. *A real, harsh reality only a continent away.*

The goggles, the controls, the environment—it felt all too much like a game at times, a terrifying simulation.

Melody's cramped hands released the controls on the arms of her chair. Her body and mind were both reluctant to abandon the alternate reality they'd been immersed in for the past four hours.

With her hands off the controls, the straps across her chest and upper arms automatically released, slithering back into their fastenings. She pulled off her goggles next and blinked at her reflection in one of the six silver metal walls of her monastic cell. Her neck cracked as she tilted her head, ear to shoulder, ear to shoulder. Then, back aching, she leaned forward to unclip the restraints on her feet

Melody pried herself from her chair only

to deposit her tired body into another one in front of a set of glowing monitors, their harsh white light the only illumination in her cell. She selected the recording of her day's mission and replayed it on mute, watching in silence the people, and more than anything, the sad, sick, starving children.

After the war ended—or at least, after the nukes stopped falling—the Sisterhood had commissioned a legion of VM's, virtual missionaries, to be sent into the devastation area where it was still too dangerous to enter. They brought their gospel, certainly, but they also brought water, food, and medicines. Some days it helped. Most days it felt like putting sunscreen on a corpse.

The last nuke had hit its mark three generations ago. The dust had settled. The sirens had stopped howling. But the world was still scarred and soon people began leaving as quick as they could, on any ship that would take them to the stars, as if the Earth itself were a leper.

Melody's avatar, a tall, lean silver robot, moved gracefully across the monitors, seeming larger than life among the children of the village where she did her missionary work. There was a certain freedom in seeing through her avatar's eyes, moving, or at least seeming to move, with its long, elegant limbs. Melody hadn't left her monastic cell in months, not since her mission had begun. All her time was split between sleep, prayer, and the godforsaken village that was her responsibility to convert and to help prosper. These people were the loneliest on Earth. Unreachable by the rest of civilization—if they could even still be counted among the civilized.

Melody's avatar was almost entirely controlled by thought. What she willed, it did. The other controls were to manage things only visible to her, that didn't exist in either reality. Using the pad of her pinkie she pressed one of the buttons on the armrest and the schematics for a modest building popped into her vision.

The building was a decontamination chamber. Via her avatar Melody guided the villagers, those who could do menial work without collapsing, through its construction. It was little more than a foundation now but once completed she would be able to travel to the village in person, her body protected from the nuclear radiation by a suit. Upon her arrival she'd enter the decontamination centre, cleanse the suit, and be able to walk around the chamber so long as the doors were kept closed. It would be a short visit, and she'd soon have to climb back into the suit and leave again, undergoing the gruelling walk across miles of flat, grey, uninhabited land back to the pick-up zone where a helicopter would be waiting to transport her back into safe, breathable air.

It will be worth it, Melody thought, looking down through the transparent blue overlay of the building schematics at the face of the little boy, Miko. He had grey skin tormented with boils and blisters so severe his left eye was almost entirely sealed shut with puss. She doubted he could see out of it at all. His black hair grew in tufts and patches around his skull which seemed overly large atop his frail, rail thin body.

The avatar's face was blank metal, the 180° sensors that transmitted back the images to Melody were buried in the sides of its head where ears ought to be. It projected Melody's voice but it came out clipped and over-processed. It was incapable of capturing or reflecting her emotions, but when she smiled down at Miko, he smiled back.

Melody adored watching the children play as it was such a rare sight. Her avatar sat on a set of steps that stood alone in the middle of the village, the building they had once led up to blown away in the original blast many years ago. The children stood in a circle, hands clasped, and 'ran' (their running was a series of cautious hop-like steps) in a circle. They had taken one of the prayers Melody had taught them and turned it into a song, a rhyme of sorts that they sang as they ran and when the chorus came to an end, they fell to the ground slowly, like browned leaves in the Fall.

Melody didn't mind how they used the prayer, though it was unconventional and perhaps, some might say, blasphemy. There were many things the villagers didn't understand about the theology of the Sisterhood. They had not been educated in generations, their language had developed into a new, unique dialect, and religion had been totally unknown to them before her coming. But they learnt. They took up prayers and ritual, they listened to her read scripture and history—even their own history about what this place had been like before the war, about who they had been. Buildings, now foundations if not complete rumble, had touched the clouds. The economy had been one of the largest on Earth. Tycoons and millionaires and even kings had called it home once. And ordinary people too. Families, schools, hospitals.

Tears streaked down Melody's cheek, blurring the images of the village. Her avatar stood and she directed it toward the decontamination chamber, lifting her goggles briefly to wipe away the tear before restoring her sight.

The chamber was complete now, it had been for four days, but it needed to sit and re-pressurize. She'd gathered the whole village around her that day and explained to them as clearly as she could that absolutely no one was permitted to enter the chamber for four days and four nights or else the toxins within could be deadly once she arrived. The villagers, her flock, had watched with their wide, sunken eyes and nodded and nodded until she'd said the whole thing through three times and then had them recite it back to her like a mantra, needing to be certain they understood.

Her request had been obeyed and it was time for the final test.

Noticing Melody's actions and curious as to her doings, villagers began to gather around again. She showed them how to operate the panels on the three doors, how one must be opened and closed behind before the next can be gone through. They watched in awed silence, occasionally poking one another. This proved they were very excited, for touching wasn't something they did often, for fear of leaving dark purple bruises on each other's frail flesh.

Once inside the chamber Melody used her armrest controls, instructing the avatar to run an air quality and radiation test.

Numbers flashed into her vision, appearing as if projected on to the inner walls of the chamber.

Melody, half a world away, strapped into a chair and peering through the eyes of a machine, held her breath.

A moment later the test came back clear. The chamber was ready. She was ready.

Melody's avatar stood on the steps facing her flock. Around its neck hung one of the brown ponchos the villagers wore. It had been hastily given and hung awkwardly, looking more like a cape than a poncho. She held her arms aloft and spoke.

"Fellow children of God." Her halting voice was amplified for the crowd to hear. "I am coming to you in a matter of days, in my own body. I'll come to see your lovely faces with my own eyes, to hold your poor, little hands in my own. I come to bestow on you my love and care in all the same ways I have done through this—" and the avatar gestured down at its own body— "and in all the other ways in which this form has restricted me."

The avatar took a step down toward the people.

"I bring with me the words and gospel. May God walk among us."

Melody closed her tear-filled eyes and pulled off her goggles.

Body and soul back in her monastic cell, she sat up and, for the first time in months, left her room.

Some of her sisters were already waiting for her in the departure room. They helped her into the suit. The metal giant looked a lot like her avatar but bigger in order to accommodate her body within. She climbed in and the suit closed around her, each finger encased in solid metal to protect her from the elements and from the radiation.

She clambered awkwardly into the helicopter. The pilots' suits were soft and not nearly so insulated, but they would be spending mere minutes in the radiation area, and nowhere near the nucleus, as she would be.

The flight was long and travelling across open water terrified her, but she had only to think back to her flock and how brave they were, how fearless and persistent, and her heart was softened.

The landing zone was a scorched patch of earth on the rim of the nuclear drop. The co-pilot helped her from the craft and no sooner had her feet touched the ground than the helicopter was disappearing into the sky.

Melody turned toward her destination.

There was nothing on the horizon but a vague grey line of destruction. Controls in the hands of the suit similar to those back on her chair brought up a map and compass. With her vitals looking good, but for a spike in anxiety, and her coordinates plugged in, she started off in the direction of the village. Her village. Her people. Her flock. She would bring God to them, if it was the last thing she did.

Miko was swinging his frail body across the monkey bars when the God arrived.

She was taller and thicker than the Prophet, but there was still a lean elegance to her movements. Long strides brought her to the edge of the village. She stood under a warped metal arch, the Eternal Abyss stretching out behind her. The cracked earth, which Miko knew stretched on forever and ever, met a blank, colourless sky at the horizon. The sun was just setting, the orange gas that rose from the Eternal Abyss masking it and turning the star an angry shade. Violent orange light shone off the God's silver carapace.

Miko was captivated by the figure the God struck, standing there at the door to his home. She had come here. Here!

His arms grew tired and the rusted metal

of the monkey bars bit into his already blistered palms. He let go, slowly dropping himself to the ground. A layer of flesh and puss was left behind, unnoticed by Miko who was so used to the deteriorating, near decomposing, state of his own body. He ran with the other children who had also noticed the God's coming, toward the metal being on the cusp of entering their village.

The children, all weak, ran with slow, gangly movements, like a horde of infantile apes just finding their legs. But their frailty could do nothing to diminish their excitement. A God, here! Here!

The God, in her limitless wisdom, knelt on one knee to accept the little ones.

Oh, how this God humbles herself before us, mere children! Miko thought, awaiting his turn in the deity's embrace.

He waited in the horde of thin children for his turn to for a hug. A long wait as the God acted with extreme care not to jar or squish the children, almost as if her limbs were not quite her own, as if she did not know her own strength.

And surely neither can we know her strength! Miko thought. Her strength is beyond understanding.

Finally, he approached the outstretched arms, the upturned palms, the blank, smooth silver face. Her carapace was warm and hard. Her very skin hummed beneath his fingers. When he pulled away, he saw the sticky puss fingerprints he left behind on her shoulders and was for a moment horrified at how he'd sullied her but if she felt his filthy marks she pretended not to notice.

Merciful and beautiful and just!

By the time the God had hugged each of the children in turn the rest of the village had gathered. They stood around, some with heads bowed others with hands raised as they muttered phrases of welcome or rehearsed prayers passed down to them by the prophet.

The God looked up at the gathering and rose to both feet again. She turned her head slowly on a sturdy neck, looking at the children in turn before holding out a hand toward Miko, the setting orange sun twinkling off the peaks of her silver digits.

Miko, a blush filling his hollow cheeks, ran forward to take her large, heavy hand in his.

"Take me to the decontamination chamber," the God said. Her voice was smoother than that of the prophet yet still jagged and far away sounding, like a hollered phrase down a long, empty hall. They had many such halls in the village buildings, the ones that had been caved in during the Devastation, and Miko smiled at the thought of this God perhaps playing with him and the other children in these haunts, her divine voice calling out Marco and Polo.

Does God giggle? Miko wondered as he led her toward the decontamination chamber, the structure her prophet had overseen construction on, the place they called the Temple.

One of the adults, little taller than Miko and not quite coming to the God's shoulder, hurried ahead and began the ritual door blessing. The sequence had to be followed perfectly—so it had been foretold by the prophet.

Nearly a third of the village entered through the three consecutive Doors of Purification, all the people that could fit in the Temple at once. The God let go of Miko's light grasp on her fingers and shooed him back gently, along with the other children who had been floundering around her legs bidding for her attention or another touch of her quick-silver skin.

Most of the children stepped back, those that didn't were pulled to their mother's tummies, held firm by hands that feared and worshipped God and her commands. Miko, obeying the order to step back, but, being her chosen guide to the Temple, allowed himself to stay just a half a step closer to the God than the others, watched in awesome wonder as she began to hiss.

An accompanying hiss echoed from the walls of the Temple. Mother's held babes tot heir chests, children cried out. Miko starred and starred as the hissing grew louder and the room filled with a light fog that dissipated almost as soon as it was gone. The God stepped forward—no, half of her stepped forward! The front of her body disconnected from the back, tilting forward and cracking her open along the seems of her very soul. Miko saw a shadowed form within. The form moved, writhed. It stepped forward, out of the God and onto the Temple floor.

The empty gaze of the God starred at the ground, emotionless, voiceless, immobile.

The thing that came out of her was pink and pale and bald, it's face fat and soft. Dew clung to it's barely-there brow and its bones were hardly visible beneath it's gooey flesh.

It had a mouth like a bug; an oval, white, toothless maw. It breathed deeply, it's chest, with two protruding swollen breasts, heaved up and down. Up. And down.

It gulped air like any greedy flesh and blood creature. This was no God perfected body of silver or steel. This thing that stood before Miko was a man—though none the like of which he'd ever seen or known to exist.

Somewhere, a child cried.

"It killed her," someone said.

Miko could all but feel the agreement of the crowd. Heads bobbed slowly, then faster...then a little faster.

"You killed God." It was whispered but shook the people like a scream.

"You killed God! You killed God!" The chant was taken up by every throat in the Temple with the capacity for noise.

The pink, gooey man's eyes widened as round as the sun and it stepped backward, just and inch but enough to knock into the God's still standing corpse.

The corpse teetered then began to topple. The crowd gasped as one, sounding much like the hiss that had issued from the walls moments before. They surged forward like a sand storm from the Abyss and swept over the pink man in their haste to catch the falling God. Catch her they did, and more than twenty calloused and blistered hands held her from the grim of the ground.

A silent agreement was made, and the mob made for the doors.

"No," croaked a small voice out of the trampled body of the God killer. "Don't open the..."

The processional marched on, through each of the Doors of Purification, out into the twilight and toward the Garden, which had been something called a Tea Room before the Devastation but within whose skeleton glass walls now nurtured many tasty leaves and sweet flowers. Miko walked, back bent, beneath the corpse of the God until the procession halted before a metal slab. The slab, shaped nearly like that of the wing of a giant bird, had been dug from the cracked earth of the Abyss and become the final resting place of the Prophet. His slim silver body laid on it's back on the slab, raised only a foot or two from the ground by two of the small white metal boxes they sometimes found food in, food from ancient times. His hands were folded on his chest, long fingers interlaced. Some of the sweetest flowers had been picked daily and set at his feet.

The twin on the metal bird's wing was brought along with more white boxes, and a new slab was erected for the God. She was laid down gently by many hands upon the slab. When her body was horizontal again her two halves slid shut. For a moment Miko dared to hope they had restored her, and it seemed the crowd shared his hope, for many minutes no one dared to move or breath.

Hope was extinguished in Miko first, as it often is with children who have little patience and the ability to replace old dreams with new faster than light reaches the retina. He picked a handful of tiny orange flowers from crack in the glass of the Garden wall and set them at the feet of the dead God.

The villagers, one by one, even those who had not been in the Temple at the time of the vicious murder, knelt before the two free standing tombs. Some mumbled, some prayed. Miko bowed his head and thought very, very hard about God and Death and Perfection before raising his head and glancing though the windows of the Garden toward the playground.

He slunk out the back, as quietly as he could, and began again his pursuit of the monkey bars.

FRAGILE

I feel air rush past my nose and pivot to my right just in time to avoid the stick that displaced it. Unfortunately, I'm not quick enough to avoid the other end.

Crack.

I gasp. I can already feel a long welt swelling across my shoulders. I spin again, but I'm too slow getting my own stick up, and my opponent lands another blow.

Crack.

That's two hits with the blue end; the weighted end that awards you more points. I grind my teeth and lunge, putting the orange end of my stick before me. She may have earned a couple valuable hits, but she took a risk; she'll have to change her stance if she wants to start hitting me with the other end. If I can keep coming at her fast enough, I might be able to claim enough orange hits to outdo her two blue ones.

She blocks me, and our sticks meet.

Crack.

I lunge again. She swings. Lunge, swing, block. Lunge, swing, block. We're both giving it our all, but we've fallen into a rhythm. She's trying to tire me. I let her think that it's working—*mostly because it is*—and I wait for my moment.

She lunges, and instead of swinging to block I fall into a low squat, letting the stick pass over my head. Her momentum carries her off balance. Sloppy. She shouldn't have relied on my block. I swing up, not letting my opportunity slip by, and slap my stick against her back, orange side first. She stumbles and lets go of her stick with one hand. I swing again and deliver two blows in quick succession to her torso. She doubles over in pain — but she's still got a hold of her stick.

I spin my stick end over end and strike again at the same spot on her torso, blue end first.

Crack. Crack. Crack.

She hisses and falls to her knees. I lunge after but she looks back at me and throws her stick to the side. I'm not sure whether the look in her eyes is defiance or defeat. The tears make it hard to tell.

A dropped weapon means the duel is over. I landed just enough blows to tie us up. Not good enough.

"Guts, Evony. Guts!" I can see the teeth in Teppo's smile while he says the praise. I bow my head and hold my stick out to him, orange end held in my left palm, blue end resting on the back of my right hand.

I hear another series of cracks. The other girls gasp, fingers raising to parted lips. They were standing around us, their lean bodies forming the duelling ring, but now they begin to huddle tighter around my felled opponent.

"Jacinth?" Teppo kneels beside her. "Are you alright?"

She's wearing only a thin, black wrapping around her breasts so it's easy to see her skin as it splits open. Long fissures open from the spot on her side where I repeatedly hit her and streak along her back and shoulders. Her skin is white marble, like mine, like all the girls our age. As it cracks open pieces begin to fall off. Then the fissures on her back meet ones that climb up her front and her entire right shoulder shatters like a dropped vase on tile. Her pastel-pink flesh is exposed to the air. As the other girls look on in horror, I look up. The moon is hidden by cloud cover. This is why girls our age only practise at night. The sun's rays would burn that sensitive under-flesh, charring it black in seconds.

"Teppo," I say, pointing to the sky with my stick.

He follows the gesture, then nods. Gray

135

patches blanket his own shoulders. He's still young, but older than us, and no stranger to the pain of Burning. He collects Jacinth in his arms, careful not to touch her exposed flesh, and carries her inside the temple.

We know better than to follow. The temple is sacred, for the masters and their apprentices only. And for the Burned.

A stinging sensation runs up my arm and I'm surprised to find a crack of my own, running from my elbow to my neck. A gray smoke is rising from the wound. I should find cover, but I stay a moment longer and look up again. The clouds have blown past. The moon is bright and full and white. I put a hand over as much of the wound as I can and follow the rest of the girls back to our beds.

There are no windows in our barracks, but the midday heat is warm. There is a small gap in the ceiling where one of the silver leaves has fallen off. I look at the stretch of pale light it casts on the floor, not joining the other girl's conversation. They're talking about putting out the sun.

"We are like beasts," Ty says, using her bunk as a soapbox. "We've been turned nocturnal. We share our time with things that crawl and creep!"

There's a soft chorus of affirmations and unanimous nodding.

"Predators are nocturnal," I say it quietly, but Ty hears me.

"Predators who stock and sneak. We are warriors—not snakes."

Snakes aren't nocturnal, they adjust to their environment, finding shade or a warm rock depending on the temperature. They're cold-blooded and versatile. We are just like snakes. But I don't tell Ty this.

She takes my silence as submission, puffing out her chest and continuing her sermon. "If we could put out the light of the sun then we could practice at all hours. Fear of Burning would be eliminated."

The other girls cheer, and I resolve to let them have their myths. Every night, some girl stands on her bunk and retells one of the many legends of the Sun that Set Forever. They listen and let their hearts thump and spirits rise, determination flooding their veins to run side-long with their blood. They know it's nothing but fairy tales, but they dream anyway.

I've stopped dreaming. Dreams are for children. I've determined that if I can not put out the sun then I will stand in it. The orb in the sky will not determine my passions.

Around me, girls climb under thin bed sheets and drift into sleep. I stay up, watching the strip of sunlight on the earthen floor. When the snoring and the sleep murmuring begins, I slip from my bunk and walk to the light. I hold my hand under it. My skin shines like midnight stars. I stretch further, bringing my elbow under the light. It sizzles when it touches the crack, but doesn't steam. The wound isn't that bad, yet. I know I should go to the temple, so I can lay on my back, dosed in ointments and bandages, bedridden for days.

I return to my bunk and lay on my uninjured shoulder.

Ty envisions bathing the world in darkness. I yearn to find my place in the sun.

Jacinth returns a fortnight after her injury. Her skin has healed but there is a light gray patch where the damage occurred. She is Shadowed now. The other girls pat her on the back and praise her bravery.

We practise with the boys today and Jacinth has worn an even scanter chest wrapping than usual to show off as much of her Shadowed shoulder as she can. The boys are impressed and

I watch as they nudge each other in line, pointing and smiling stark white teeth.

I wear a top that starts high on my neck and stops just below my meagre breasts. It goes to my wrist on one side, covering my cracked arm, and is sleeveless on the other. I've even donned a pair of full black leggings. It's hot this evening, and I look foolish wearing so much fabric, but it will cover any new cracks I might receive while duelling the boys.

We're waiting under one of the Shades, a massive willow whose canopy is thick enough to keep out all light, even in the day. The Shades grow in the valley between the Twins. The ground is hard here and the roots of the Shades have to reach far down to suck up the moisture from the mountain rivers in the caves below. I've never been to the earth below the Twins. The two mountain peaks keep us safe from enemies and bandits yet bring us closer to the sun. A weighty compromise.

Teppo steps between our lines, holding a duelling stick across his shoulders. "Fair fighting tonight, everyone. I don't want to have to make any temple runs."

We spread out, creating a large circle beneath the Shade. Teppo holds the duelling stick out with one hand, pointing to us each in turn as he walks backwards around the circle, meeting our eyes, looking for nervous grins or fidgeting fingers. I make sure to give him both, and they aren't entirely disingenuous. My excitement is hard to contain. I'm anxious to put my plan into motion, the sooner the better.

"Evony," he says. "And Coal. You two are up first."

I step into the circle with my duelling stick and Coal steps in across from me. He's a tall boy, with dark hair and bottomless eyes. His parents gave him a good, dark name. His father is one of the darkest Shadowed in our village and Coal has already earned a few gray patches of his own. From what I've heard he likes to fight with the other boys outside of practice and often gets reprimanded. He's not a mean boy, but he doesn't hold his punches.

We meet in the centre of the circle and tap our duelling sticks together, my blue end meeting with his orange. I can feel the tension of my peers as Teppo retreats to the ring with them and they huddle tighter, shoulders brushing. A collective breath is held — the unspoken ritual of a mob awaiting blood. It feels like only Coal and I have remembered how to breathe.

Despite the heat, I believe for a moment that I can see his breath leaving his lips in thin wispy clouds, as it does in the cold. Huff, puff, puff in time with his heartbeat. But it's only my heart I hear. I raise my stick and will my feet to be weightless.

His arms are longer than mine and he uses his extra reach as an advantage. He strikes first, orange end held high, and brings it down toward me. I should block, hold my stick up horizontally against his attack, but I take the hit, getting the brunt of it on my good shoulder. Meanwhile, I strike his left thigh, exposed by his aggressive stance. I strike his other hip as he pivots to get away from the surprise blow.

I spin well away from him just in case he lunges for me. He doesn't. My move was risky so he's being careful now. He takes up a defensive stance with his feet planted firmly beneath his shoulders, knees bent, and the blue end of his stick on his right shoulder.

My heart is racing and despite the tension, I laugh. He smiles back—and lunges for me.

I bound out of his reach and take a half-hearted swing in his direction. He dodges it with ease and beings a chase, carefully following me around the rim of the circle.

With his long legs and arms staying just out of his reach is tiring. I block every swing he takes at me but I know I can't keep up this momentum long. He thinks he has me. He can hear my ragged breathing and see the sweat on my face. He's biding his time for a blow that will knock me down.

Something in his eyes changes and I know he'll strike. He adopts an aggressive stance again, arms high, feet spread wide. As he swings at me I duck and slide on the dirt, slipping right between his legs.

I hop to my feet behind him, spinning, and hit him once, twice, three times before he spins and blocks my barrage. Our sticks meet with such force that my forearms sting. Instead of backing out of the block, Coal pushes against my stick with everything he has and sends me tumbling to the ground.

I manage a backward somersault, still holding my stick in both hands, and land in a crouch. He's coming toward me, stilling cautious.

When he's close I fake to my left, exaggerating a dodge to that side, then spin counterclockwise, jumping in the air for momentum, and bring the orange end of my duelling stick down hard on his left shoulder. He drops his stick with one hand but recovers quickly. I'm already out of his reach by then. I turn to get some more distance and find myself face to face with a row of my peers. They look like a ring of white, porcelain dolls, all wearing the same surprised expression; eyes wide and lips pressed into little O's so perfect they appear painted on.

I hesitate too long and can hear Coal's steps behind me. I've hit him too many times now, he can't afford to be cautious.

I don't have time to dodge him so I break through the circle of bodies, people scatter out of my way.

My feet slide in the dirt as I turn and take up an aggressive stance, holding my stick high. Coal follows me, but he stops just beyond the ring of students. My break from the duelling ring has put me beyond the canopy of the Shade.

I risk a glance up. The night is clear. I'm standing in a pool of moonlight.

I look back at Coal and swing my stick, hand over hand, around my waist. A stupid flourish. An opponent could easily knock the stick from my hand if they were close enough. It's a taunt. He gets the message.

He runs toward me and I don't back down. He's a few steps away when I move into his attack. I duck and spring up between his stick and his chest. I bring my own stick with me and as I spring back up I clock the side of his face with the orange end. The blow knocks him aside, his stick ripped from his hands and tossed to the ground.

His face is turned away from me and for a moment the moonlight is paralyzing. If I've cracked his face he'll Burn.

He turns to me. He's got his right hand over his cheek. He spits pink-red blood onto the ground beside him, but as he removes his hand, white fingers tinged with pink, I see that his face is intact.

Coal laughs. "Guts, Evony. Where'd that come from?"

I laugh too, letting the tension ebb away. There's a wave of chatter and sighs from the dismantled duelling ring as Teppo jogs over to us.

"Are you cracked, Coal?" Teppo asks.

Coal shakes his head. "I'm fine."

Teppo helps him to his feet before turning to me. I hold out my staff in the customary gesture. I can feel my shoulders heaving as my lungs struggle to breathe at a normal pace again.

"You take risks, Evony." He isn't looking at me. His eyes are on the moon. "Our lives depend on balance and constant caution."

"Warriors should be brave," I say under my breath. Only Coal and Teppo hear me.

"Warriors should be wise." It doesn't sound like a reprimand. He raises his hand over my duelling stick and taps one end with two fingers, then the other, testing its strength and balance. He's given me the win even though I broke the rules and left the ring.

I see Coal standing just behind him,

smiling, a ribbon of red trailing over his lip and down his white chin. I hadn't meant to beat him like that, but he didn't seem to mind.

The mountain air has turned cold. Everyone is wearing leggings now, along with thick wools and furs. I'm in a black shirt with a long neck and long sleeves that have holes for my thumbs. I've been wearing my winter clothes for weeks now, even when it was too warm. I'm gaining more cracks and if they're noticed I'll be forced to the temple to heal them, so I keep them concealed.

The sun that shines into the valley is bright, but not warm enough to keep the small lake from freezing. Little wooden huts have appeared on its surface, as they do every year at this time, to fish in around little holes cut into the ice.

As I stand on the peak of a hill looking down at the huts and the people teetering precariously across the ice, a breeze blows through the Peaks, whistling and blowing my hair in my face. I push it aside and pull my fur coat around my shoulders.

I feel a pressure against my thigh and look down to see the head of a little white goat pressing against it.

"Hello, Surefoot."

The white goat takes a few steps backwards on the hill, then runs at me again, head butting my leg. I'm prepared for the blow so he doesn't knock me off my feet, though it does sort of hurt. But I'd decided shortly upon making my acquaintance with Surefoot that I wouldn't let the ill-tempered little mammal get to me. So, after his next assault, I smile and pat him fondly between his alabaster horns.

Apparently, he took my kindness as a further insult because he begins chewing on my coat. Well, the joke is on him because I hate this coat.

The long, brown fur coat is a relic of my childhood. A pampered, pristine, childhood. I'd sound like a spoiled brat if I complained, so I don't. Not out loud. The truth is if I could have traded my lot with someone worse off I'd have done it in a heartbeat. My mother always called me her little doll and promised she'd never let anything happen to me, ever. And she'd kept that promise. I didn't leave my own house until I was seven. I wasn't permitted to walk on my own outdoors until I was ten, and even then I was accompanied at all times by babysitters who looked more like they should have been guarding an emperor than a little girl. School was a new kind of torment. I wasn't permitted to play with the other children. Sitting next to them in class was my only peer interaction.

That, and the comments, name-calling, and glares they dished out at every opportunity.

All children are white, to a degree, but accidents, especially while roughhousing with siblings or friends, are impossible to avoid. Every child has shade spots here and there, whether it be a broken arm, a blow from a duelling stick, or busted knees from falling out of a tree. Every child that is, but me. I was pristine white with not so much as a sliver of shade on my skin. For this, I was tormented. I was considered weak, fragile. All through school I was told by teachers how young I looked because they couldn't believe a girl my age had lasted so long without a single shade spot.

When graduation came and we decided what we wanted to pursue, I chose to become a warrior. The decision was at the total horror and contempt of my parents, but a warrior gave up everything. Title, money, family name — my parents didn't own me anymore.

I was given one gift from them upon leaving home. This coat. My mother couldn't hold me and wrap me in her protective, smothering grasp anymore. Maybe she thought the coat could somehow replace her. I kept it because it was warm, and throwing it out would be spiteful and childish. Besides, it is a beautiful coat, even if I did hate what it represented.

"Nice coat."

The voice startles me and I jump, nearly tripping over Surefoot. I regain my balance and turn to find Coal, smiling.

"Nice goat too," he says.

"Oh, it's not mine."

"Well, it's attached to you."

I look down. Surefoot is still nibbling at the fur despite me almost kicking him right off the hill. "Yeah, well..."

Surefoot abandons the coat and goes over to Coal. I figure he'll give him the customary head butt, but he just nuzzles gently at Coal's knee. Coal pats him on the head and Surefoot makes a pleased bleating sound.

"He's friendly," Coal says.

I roll my eyes and turn back to look down at the lake.

"You want to go for a walk?" Coal asks. "My brother has a hut, it's not much to see but it's kind of neat if you've never been in one."

I look at him again in surprise. He seems bashful then, looking down at his feet.

"I know they usually send us off to train someplace away from our families but, well, I have a big family. We're spread out all over the Peaks."

"Oh, it's not that," I say.

He's silent for a moment. "So, what is it?"

It's just that I think you might be hitting on me and I have no idea how to reciprocate, or if I should, or if I want to, and I'm beginning to panic!

I take a deep breath. "I've never been in a fishing hut before. I'd love to see one."

He seems relieved by this and gives me another smile. I hadn't noticed before how big he smiled and how much it changed his face. His eyes get smaller but brighter, and his cheeks round like he's holding water in his mouth.

As we walk down the hill toward the lake I get wondering what my face looks like when I smile. Does it light up too? Or does it warp into some horribly grotesque arrangement? I decide not to smile again just in case. Not until I find out if I look like a mountain goat when I grin.

I've had to add socks and gloves to my black wardrobe. The only skin I allow to show is my face and even so, I keep my black hair long, bangs covering much of my forehead. Other's take my excessive coverings to be a form of penance, like the religious wear in the temples. I know they believe I do it out of guilt. And I know they believe Coal is my crime. No one suspects I'm hiding a broken body.

I sit on my bunk and retie the white wrapping around my knee. I've shattered it so many times that I need the wrap just to keep the pieces from falling off. Each time I find I have to tie it tighter and tighter. This time it's so tight that when I stand I can barely feel my toes. I go to the window of my hut and look out over the moonlit mountains. I was given this hut upon the completion of my training. I'm a trainer myself now, but I think the kids are a little bit frightened of me.

Surefoot is my only roommate now. He's an old goat with a long silver goatee and one broken horn. He looks about as ragged as I feel. He butts his head against my leg, avoiding my damaged knee. The familiar abuse of the grumpy old animal is comforting. I pat his head and lean against the window sill.

I don't know how long I stare out at the grey and blue peaks but Coal has snuck in quietly while I've been distracted and I jump a little as he wraps his arms around my waist. I can feel his smile as he props his chin on my shoulder. The left side of his face is entirely Shadowed from a blow he received a few years ago. It's been a week since I've seen that face and I'm glad he's back from patrol. I settle back against him, relishing the warmth and strength of his embrace.

This is the extent of our relationship. I let others believe otherwise, but Coal and I took vows upon choosing the warriors path and we have no intention of breaking them.

"How was patrol?" I ask, still watching the mountains. I'm getting sleepy and the sky is getting light. I think about curling up on my cot with Coal beside me and my eyelids feel even heavier.

"Cold," he says. "How's your knee?"

Coal knows I refuse to use the temple. He doesn't ask why. He knows I'm a good warrior and doesn't question my methods. But he also doesn't know how broken I've become, how damaged my body is. Maybe then he would worry, tell me I'm pushing myself too hard, insist on me going to the temple. So even with him, I remain covered.

I'm about to tell him my knee is just fine when I see a light on the horizon. It's not the sun. It's a brilliant orange glow, confined to a hilltop.

"Coal..."

A long screeching echoes between the peaks. A death whistle. The call of the warriors. More fires are lit atop the mountain hills, the war forges.

Coal releases me. I turn to him and see the glowing mountain fires reflected in his black marble eyes.

"The Enemy is coming."

There are only a few hours till sunrise. The ranks of warriors are amassed between the peaks as we await our adversary. The Enemy has adapted to climbing mountains or to fighting at this altitude. They have most likely lost many of their ranks getting here, but reports say a good portion have made it and are nearing the summit. Were it night we would have no problem fighting off the weakened opponent, but the sun is rising too and any injury we take will be open to the morning rays. Burning is a crippling pain, impossible to fight through. A simple crack could drop one of the finest among us.

I can tell by the tension in the warriors around me that they are all thinking the same thing, calculating the same odds.

For now, we are the reinforcements. Coal is standing beside me. He moves his spear to his left hand and grabs my hand with his right, squeezing my gloved fingers. In silence, we watch the ranks of warriors ahead of us march into battle.

The Enemy is crawling over the distant mountain ridge. They're too far away to see clearly but I've seen their likenesses immortalized in a mural on our temple walls. They're quadrupedal, with bodies much larger than ours. They have powerful back legs that are almost frog-like, but they prowl like big cats and have a scream and long sharp teeth to match. Theirs have massive hunched backs with a row of sharp protruding spikes of bone. They run on all fours but when they fight they rise on two legs and swing with a deadly, skin cracking force.

They meet our first rank as the sky turns a fleshy pink.

I grab Coal's hand tighter and pull him aside.

"Where are we going?" he asks, as we slink away from the army.

"We aren't going to win."

Coal stops, yanking his hand from mine. His jaw is set. "I'm not running from this battle."

I take his hand again. "We aren't abandoning them. Just trust me."

I feel resistance at first as I continue walking away, but then his arm goes slack and he follows.

One of the war forges is lit not far from

the reinforcement troops. Four pillars surround it, and steps lead down on all four sides to the fiery pit in the centre.

"What are we doing here?" Coal asks.

I bend forward and unwrap the white fabric around my knee and let it fall to the stones. Then I start removing my clothes.

Coal watches in growing horror as my wounds are revealed. There are cracks up and down my shoulders, criss crossing over my back and trailing down and around my legs. Even my hands and toes have tiny cracks like a broken glass bowl that's been tediously glued back together. My knee, now free of its wrapping, shatters and falls to the ground with a snap. My whole kneecap, gone, and raw pink flesh exposed.

I turn to Coal. His eyes are wide. He's silent and not moving. I can see the battlefield over his shoulder and we aren't winning. Soon they will be upon the reinforcements.

"Hit me," I say.

"What?"

"Hit me. Break my face."

"Evony, what are you talking about? You can't fight like this. You've got to go to the temple—"

"In an hour we won't have a temple, Coal. Please. I have a plan, and it might not work but you've got to help me try."

Coal takes a step back but something changes his mind. I see it in the way he's set his jaw again, like when he thought I was going to desert. Determination. Even in the face of evident failure.

He nods, takes an offensive stance, and swings.

I keep my footing and take the blow. Then the next one, and the next one. I don't know if it's the force or the pain that brings me to my knees but I find myself on the ground, staring at the stones, the fire burning off to my left. I wait for another blow but it doesn't come. Then I hear it. A snapping. All along my spine the cracks are spreading and growing wider. Pieces star breaking and falling off, hitting the stones. It sounds like someone is breaking dishes against a wall. I can feel the cold air against my exposed skin and know that soon the sun will be high enough to touch it. Out between the peaks, far from the temple or huts or the Shade trees, I have nowhere to hide.

My face hurts where Coal repeatedly struck me. Where I've never taken damage before. I move my jaw.

CRACK.

My face falls off in one big chunk of white. It doesn't shatter against the stones but just lays there like a mask. I pick it up between raw, red hands, and hold it to my face. I look out of the eyes that I'd called my own for so long. The holes through which I saw the world. I put it down again, leaving tiny red fingerprints on the cheeks and forehead.

I stand, now even more naked than before. Coal says something to me but it's drowned out by distant battle cries and my own raging adrenaline. I step down toward the fire. Only four more steps between me and the orange-red flames.

Coal is screaming for me to stop.

I step into the flames. My flesh is burning, burning far beyond anything the sun or moon could inflict. I see white and for a moment I think it's hot flame but it's just the heat against my eyes. I can't tell if they're open or closed. I'm screaming too, until the flames get in my mouth to silence me. I drop to the floor of the pit, trying to stay conscious, not sure if I'm managing it.

I can't hear Coal anymore. I can feel the pain but I'm senseless. My body is twitching and I'm starting to feel...something. Stronger. Cooler. Like a barrier is forming between my skin and the flames.

Temple treatments typically consist of hot

ointments or salves that slowly and gently burn the skin, sealing cracks and leaving the skin Shaded, but stronger.

The hotter the burn the stronger the repaired flesh. But most can't handle anything beyond a mild burn.

This is far beyond mild. This is far beyond the most extreme treatments of the temple.

I manage to hold a hand up in front of my face. My skin is returning, a thin lacquer coating my flesh in white. It's getting thicker every second and the flames are getting easier to bear.

I pull myself up and find the steps, crawling at first I can get my feet under me. I step from the flames back onto the stones. Coal is still standing there. He's so close to the edge of the pit it surprises me. He grabs me and pulls me from the fire.

My skin must be hot because he lets go quickly, patting his hands against his thighs.

"What were you going to do?" I ask, my voice raspy. "Go in after me?"

He laughs and shakes his head. "I can't believe you're alive. And look at you!"

I do and find pristine white skin. I look like a newborn, but I'm intact and I feel stronger than ever.

Coal removes his black shirt and gives it to me. I discarded my clothes too close to the flames and in my struggle to get out I must have pushed them into the pit to be incinerated. His shirt only comes to my thighs, but it will have to do. I grab my spear and sprint toward the battlefield. Coal is close behind me.

The Enemy swarms between the peaks, attacking our ranks, their cries echoing off the cliffs. As Coal and I get closer one of the Enemy notices us and starts galloping in our direction. I stop, planting my bare feet in the snow. My skin is still so hot that I've left melted prints behind me and I can feel it melting beneath my feet as I lock into a defensive stance, one foot firmly before the other. The ground shakes as my opponent approaches. I can see that its black body is covered in shaggy, matted hair which I assume is the source of the offensive smell it's bringing with it.

Two feet away from me it stops, stands on its back legs, and reaching a clawed hand back to grab one of the bone spikes along its spine. It rips one straight out of its back with a roar and brandishes it before him like a club.

That bone is strong—the strongest material known to us. We have some relics of times past when we used to conduct raids on the Enemy; long bones displayed in the temple on wooden pedestals. Trophies from a time we don't remember. It's strong enough to shatter us to pieces so they must be avoided at all costs.

I block the Enemy's first assault with the shaft of my spear. My arms shake from the force. I have just enough time to dive into the snow to my left out of the way of its second attack. I sidestep away from the beast, spinning my spear over my head for momentum. I can see Coal coming up behind the Enemy, spar raised.

"Coal, don't,"

My warning alerts the creature to the danger behind it and it turns. I don't waste the opportunity. Rather than attempting a close proximity attack, I throw my spear, plunging it into the tough, hairy flesh of its breast. It screams but doesn't drop its weapon. It takes a dying swing toward Coal but he stays out of reach. The Enemy falls in the snow. Coal approaches slowly to make certain it's dead.

"We've got to get into the heart of the fighting," I say, looking at the white bodies piling up not far from me.

I leave my spear in the Enemy and take up its weapon instead. It's not as heavy as I assumed. I test my nail against its curved length and I can feel its strength.

The battle rages on and I march toward it. Coal is at my side as we face two more of the beasts at the edge of the battlefield. Coal throws his spear and lands a direct hit to one of the beasts, the spear piercing its throat as it roars. I get closer to my target and manage to get in a blow to its head before it can free another of the spikes from its back. The hit crushes its skull. The feeling of shattering bone is satisfying. The rest of their skeletons aren't nearly as strong as those spinal spikes which mean we can use them against them.

"Evony!"

I spin to find Coal standing beneath a massive one of the beasts, at least three times his height. Coal is standing on the body of the Enemy he killed, trying to retrieve his spear but it must be stuck. I sprint to him, my heart beating, desperate to make it in time.

I almost don't.

I slide in the snow in front of Coal and I don't have time to get my weapon up before the beast brings his own down. The bone club strikes me on the back. I can feel the reverberations all through my body and I wait for my skin to crack and shatter—but it doesn't.

The forge worked. I've been reborn in flames, my skin hardened to a degree it had previously not known.

I am immune to this scourge.

Coal frees his spear from his fallen opponent's throat.

"Take those too wounded to fight to the forge," I tell Coal. "Don't force them, but tell them it's our only hope."

"You want me to tell them to walk into a pit of fire?"

"I do."

"They won't believe me."

"I'll make them."

I bound into the heart of the battle. I don't have time to argue with Coal. I just have to hope he listens and hope the rest of our people will spot me on the battlefield.

At first, I fight one Enemy at a time as they break from their horde. But the pile of black bodies around me begins to draw notice and soon I'm facing many opponents at once. I jump up onto the hill of Enemy bodies to gain some height advantage, but I know soon I'll be overwhelmed. Some warriors come to my aid, and for a time we hold them off. I risk a glance toward the forge and see a fiery figure stepping out. Coal. Of course, he'd go first. Still a man on fire he pounds his new, solid fist into one of the four pillars and it crumbles. Soon, other injured warriors are crawling into the flames.

With renewed vigour and a battle cry, I rejoin the fight.

The sky has gone from pink to blue, the morning fog burnt off hours ago. I'm sitting on the hunched back of a dead Enemy, its spinal spikes entirely used up. Around me, fresh white bodied warriors help the wounded and pull the spikes from the dead. We won't let them go to waste. They will be a welcome new weapon for our warriors.

Coal climbs up and seats himself beside me, his bloodied spear resting across his knees. His skin is new and white and sparkles in the bright midday sun. The half of his face that used to be Shaded is pristine.

"You look so young," I tell him.

He laughs. "You have always looked young. The rest of us are going to have to get used to it."

I wrap my arms around him, still wearing his shirt. He had the foresight to leave his pants far enough away from the pit not to burn up. His chest is still bare though and I lean against the new white flesh baking in the sun.

The sun.

I feel it on my skin like soft kisses, like my mother's coat, like bed sheets still warm from someone's vacated body. I tilt my face up toward the glowing orb, eyes closed.

I whisper, too soft even for Coal to hear it:
"Here I am. Fragile now more."

THE GREY PLANET

The black pebble filled Alafair's tiny palm. She admired the blue stripe that cut diagonally across its smooth surface. When she saw that her brother had noticed it, she tried to hide it, closing her fingers tightly.

"Give it to Momma," Durril said before turning his back on her to look over the horizon.

The air was thin and full of dust—not the dry kind, but a moist dust, the kind that gathers around the rims of window sills. It coated everything, mixing with the sand and turning it grey.

They weren't supposed to be out long when it blew like this. The dust would stick to all the little hairs inside their nostrils and travel down their throats like a fungus, clogging their airways. Durril coughed and pulled his thin linen scarf over his mouth and nose before continuing the trek towards home.

The sun was low, threatening to let the moons retake their dominion over the sky, but Durril knew more sinister things ruled the darkness that followed the twilight hours. He looked back at his little sister: she was petting the pebble with her small index finger.

"Give it to Momma," he repeated, this time pointing a finger at the bulky robot that followed them. It looked like a big metal barrel that had been knocked on its side. It had folding metal rods on each end for arms, and small wheels beneath it that left three parallel tracks in the dust. It had no face, but Durril often imagined the two large screws that attached the small door to its front were its eyes, and the bottom of the door a pair of pursed lips, forever pressed into an emotionless line.

Alafair pouted, but turned to the robot and opened the door, making Momma yawn. She kissed the pebble and whispered something to it before dropping it into the robot's hollow compartment. There was a blanket inside to soften the echo that otherwise would have rung out across the empty, rocky desert.

They kept moving.

"Dead one," Alafair mentioned, pointing as they passed the carcass of a Moaner. The low, four-legged creatures had powerful legs and teeth that could crack stone. This one's body was badly decomposed after rotting in the sun, but Durril could still see where it had been shredded--limbs nearly torn off, face in tatters, the wounds inflicted by another one of Satan's creations further up the food chain.

The Moaners were dangerous and quick, but their bright orange fur gave them away against the grey-scale surroundings—sunset and sunrise were the most dangerous, when they could bleed into the horizon. At night they padded around the desert in packs, howling to each other, though that wasn't where they'd got their name. When they died, when those other things came to rip them into ribbons, they cried and moaned like a woman in labor.

Durril spotted the Ant Hills just as the four white waning moons rose into the grey sky, peeking over the horizon. The Ant Hills looked like the rest of the rock formations that dotted the planet's surface, but they were artificial, made to camouflage with the terrain so that they could not be located from above. Durril often wondered if God could see them.

He brushed the wet dust away from the handle of the Anthill and opened up the hatch. Durril let Alafair jump down first, and then folded Momma's wheels and passed her sideways and down into Alafair's waiting hands. Durril took one last look at the darkening sky. The heavy cloud cover had dissipated somewhat, revealing something out of place. Four distinct lines ran across a clear patch of sky. They looked like clouds, but Durril had never seen them take such a shape before. Another cloud drifted in front, and the odd formation was hidden from him. He turned away and jumped into the hole. Alafair had turned on a flashlight, but the darkness of the tunnel still closed in when Durril shut the hatch.

They moved quickly through the tunnels that connected the Ant Hills together. Each had its own hatch into the main pods, one per family of Aunt, Uncle, and two children. Originally, the children were almost always the Aunt and Uncle's, but later they were moved to different homes depending on their skill set. Durril and Alafair weren't womb siblings, but they were both natural scavengers so the colony put them together not as siblings but as Partners. They would stay with their Aunt and Uncle until they were old enough to each get pods of their own.

When they reached the end of the tunnel, the children saw Aunt Beti sitting in one of the pod's nooks. She had a basket of string beside her and was crocheting a scarf. It wasn't very good, but she was a scavenger, not a garment maker. The poor workmanship was expected and accepted gratefully by her children whenever they were gifted with one of her projects.

Alafair turned off the flashlight once they reached the candle-lit pod. The flickering flames gave the dirt walls an ominous appearance, but candles had the virtue of being easy to make. Batteries did not.

"Where is Uncle Papin?" Alafair asked.

"He took some parts to Aunt Mill," Aunt Beti replied.

Alafair and Durril exchanged a doubtful look. Uncle Papin often stayed out too late, and everyone said it was just a matter of time before the monsters got him. While Aunt Beti wouldn't lie to them, they'd lived here long enough to know that Uncle Papin might lie to her.

Together they went into the smaller dug out room that was their shared space. Each had a bed and a cupboard to stow their few belongings.

They stripped off their musty clothes, leaving only thin leggings and tunics. Durril tucked his tunic in so it ballooned out around his waist, but Alafair left hers to hang around her thighs like a dress.

After laying her dirty garments on her bed, Alafair opened her cupboard and removed a string of perfectly round blue stones. They were rare, and how they were formed was a mystery, but they held no real value to the colony, so the children were allowed to keep the ones they found. Alafair had a knack for finding them, and when she had enough she would get one of the Uncles to drill a hole through their centers and string them on wire. She wore them around her neck, close to her throat. Durril found the bright blue to be strikingly out of place—the only color they had in their world besides the terrifically vibrant fur of the

Moaners—but Alafair considered that a valuable thing indeed.

Free of their scavenging clothes, Durril and Alafair re-entered the tunnels to travel to a larger pod in the center of the tunnel system. Located deepest beneath the earth, this massive pod had three purposes: a communal room where the children gathered to play, a meeting chamber for the adults, and a shelter safer than all the others. It had only one entrance, designed to be opened and closed from the inside only, so the colony could lock themselves in if necessary. What situation might require this was never specified.

A dark-haired boy with freckled cheeks came to greet them when they entered.

"You two are back late. Picking up your Uncle's habits?" he joked. Alafair took this as an insult and jumped to her Uncle's defense.

"Listen, poop face, you never mind what us or our Uncle are doing. Just mind your own business." She stormed off across the room, stomping her small boots against the hard dirt floor.

The boy's eyes widened as he watched her leave.

"She doesn't mean any harm, Wyatt." Durril said. "It's just that everyone's been giving him a bit of a hard time lately, you know?"

"Oh yeah, I know," Wyatt said, nodding so vigorously that his hair fell in front of his eyes. He had one curl that rested against his forehead, which Great Aunt Ziva called his Superman curl. She liked to tell stories about heroes; she especially liked the ones who went on long journeys, met mysterious strangers, and saved worlds. Aunt Beti said Ziva's mind was stuck in the past--Uncle Papin said that the past she talked about had never existed.

"What happened to your tooth?" Durril asked as he noticed Wyatt absently sticking his tongue through a gap in his grin.

"Oh, I fell on the butt of my spear chasing a Lox," he said, grinning even wider.

"That must've hurt."

"Yup, but I caught it."

"Well all's good then, I guess.

"Rabbit made fun of me," Wyatt whispered secretively.

"I would've made fun of you too," Durril said, unable to stop himself from laughing.

Wyatt pushed him playfully and Durril automatically pushed him back—he immediately regretted it. Wyatt grabbed hold of Durril's tunic and threw him to the dirt. Durril grabbed onto him too, and the boys began rolling around, each trying to get to their feet while keeping the other pinned. Wyatt was a hunter, trained to kill game and protect the colony. That meant daily battle training and muscles twice the size of the other kids. Durril was particularly scrawny, and his only hope was squirming out of reach and praying for assistance. But Wyatt had him trapped this time, pinned to the earth with his forearm across Durril's collar bone. Durril could feel the hard-packed dirt pressing up against his shoulder blades, gripping his clothes nearly as effectively as Wyatt.

Wyatt stuck his tongue out at his helpless opponent. Then Durril watched as his face flew out of view and the pressure was removed from his chest. Rabbit's face appeared above him as he gasped for breath. Hundreds of tight little braids fell around her cheeks as she looked down on him. Durril tried to smile, achieving only a squinting grimace.

"Why do I always find you lying in the dirt?" Rabbit asked, offering him a hand up.

Durril accepted and let her pull him to his feet. "Because I always pick fights with bigger people."

"That's the truth."

Wyatt was already on his feet again, having recovered from the shove Rabbit had given him. He gave Durril a friendly push, a signal of reconciliation. "You'll beat me one day,

Durril," he said before walking off to join some other boys. Durril doubted that.

He turned back to Rabbit. Alafair stood beside her, clutching the hand of the older girl. The candle light brought out the golden tones in Rabbit's dark brown skin, but it made Alafair's face look even paler than it was—eyes sunken in their sockets, hollow cheeks filled with shadows. Durril thought the contrast was appropriate, considering what the two girls thought of the tunnels. Rabbit called them home, but little Alafair, only just turned six, hated them with every fiber of her tiny being. He hoped she would grow out of it—but then, he hadn't, so why should she?

"Did you see the clouds today?" Durril asked Rabbit.

"Hard not to. The whole sky was clouds."

"I mean did you see the weird clouds?"

Rabbit looked down at Alafair.

"If you're telling secrets, I want to hear," Alafair said, squeezing her hand.

Rabbit looked back at Durril who nodded. Despite being five years younger, Alafair was his Partner, and he wouldn't keep things from her. Also, she was too smart and would probably find out anyway.

"I saw them," Rabbit admitted.

"The four lines?"

"Contrails."

"What are those?" Alafair asked.

"Engines leave them." Rabbit replied.

"Something was flying above the planet today?" Durril asked.

"Most likely in our atmosphere, but yes."

"Did you tell the adults?"

"Of course."

"And?"

Rabbit bit her lip. "They sent out a scout."

"Who?"

"Uncle Papin," Alafair said. "He's not bringing parts to Aunt Mill."

Durril looked to Rabbit for confirmation. She nodded.

"When did they send him?"

"Late this morning. Wyatt and I spotted them just after we left and came back to report. Then they had a short meeting, and he left."

"What was he supposed to do? Follow the lines all day?" Durril asked.

"They think whatever caused them landed

here."

"He hasn't come back yet."

"He'll show up," Rabbit said.

"He'll get eaten by Moaners," Alafair said.

"Alafair!" Durril chided.

"Or whatever eats Moaners," she continued more quietly.

"No one is getting eaten," Durril said. "He'll be back soon."

He took Alafair's hand from Rabbit and led her back to their pod. She didn't protest. Usually they would have a game of marbles before bed, but tonight neither of them felt like playing. And the more Durril thought about his Uncle Papin, the more tired he felt. He would go to bed early tonight and hope morning came quickly.

All night long, Durril listened to the Moaners conversing on the surface, just meters above his head. Alafair hadn't slept either, and they had spent the night looking at each other through the faint light of the candle that Aunt Beti left flickering on the table in the main pod.

When the electric lights finally came on, signifying that it was just before dawn, Durril and Alafair jumped from their beds, threw on their clothes, and hurried to join Aunt Beti in the main pod for breakfast.

She hummed a tuneless song as she placed two bowls of steaming porridge down in front of them. Neither picked up their spoons.

"Aunt Beti, where is Uncle Papin?" Durril asked.

"Gone to the parts pod with Uncle Rew. They're helping the construction team find good parts for the new windmill." She smiled, and placed the milk in front of them on the table.

Alafair scrunched up her nose at it. It was bitter, made from a bean they farmed on the surface. It seemed that nothing grown from the grey dirt was capable of sweetness.

Aunt Beti kissed them both and told them to be careful, before heading to the parts room herself for the weekly inventory check. Caution wasn't something she typically reminded them of, and the partners exchanged another knowing look. She was lying to them.

They ate the rest of their breakfast and Alafair went to Momma, who was sitting beside the entrance to the tunnel. She opened the little door to make sure Aunt Beti had emptied her as usual, and then reached her hand under the belly of the robot to find the on–switch. When flipped, Momma would spring to life, and gain the ability to sense their presence and follow them without much instruction.

"Wait, Alafair," Durril said, stopping her hand. "We aren't bringing Momma today."

"Why not?" She looked at him, puzzled.

"I want to go look for Uncle Papin. Momma will slow us down." Momma would also show their GPS signal to Aunt Beti and the others.

Alafair stood up and placed her hands on her hips. "Alright, but I'm taking my knife."

She was referring to the tiny stone blade Rabbit had made for her—the one Aunt Beti always made her leave behind. Durril thought Wyatt was probably the only one who could manage even scratching something with such a pitiful weapon, but it made Alafair feel brave and special.

"Fine," Durril agreed.

Alafair ran into their room and came back with the knife and one of the ribbons of cloth she used to keep her dirty blond hair out of her face. She threaded the cloth through the hole in the end of the knife's wooden handle and tied it tightly to the leather belt that kept her baggy linen pants around her waist rather than around her ankles.

"Don't stab yourself with that thing," Durril said.

"Yes, Aunty," she replied, dragging out the title in a condescending tone accompanied by the dramatic three-sixty of her light grey eyes.

Durril ignored her attitude and headed for the tunnel—but not the one leading to the hatch.

"Where are we going?" Alafair hurried to catch up.

"That knife of yours isn't going to do us much good if we find hostiles on whatever landed here," Durril said.

Alafair pouted, but followed Durril through the maze of tunnels until they arrived at the entrance to an identical pod. They stopped a few steps back from the entrance and waited to be spotted. Rabbit was sitting on a bench directly in front of them lacing up a pair of thick leather boots. When she noticed them she quickly finished her task and joined them in the tunnel.

"What's up?" she asked with a smile.

"I need you to come with us. We're going to find Uncle Papin," Durril explained.

Her smile disappeared. She peeked back

into the pod to make sure her Aunt and Uncle weren't watching, and then she grabbed Durril's arm and dragged him farther into the tunnel, Alafair following close behind.

"Are you crazy?" Rabbit whispered harshly.

"He hasn't come back, and someone needs to find out what's going on. I know the adults won't send anyone else. They won't risk it," Durril whispered back.

"My job is to protect this colony, Durril, and yours is to find things we can use and bring them back to the colony. We can't go out gallivanting around the whole planet on some wild Lox chase!"

"If there is a crashed ship out there, then it could have an infinite amount of resources we could use. Me and Alafair are going out there to do our jobs, and we're part of this colony too—so, if you let us go alone, unprotected, you're not doing your job." He jutted out his chin with a confidence he didn't feel.

She narrowed her eyes at him and he stared back doggedly, crossing his arms over his chest. After a far too long minute, she sighed and nodded.

"But Wyatt can't come." Alafair added.

"I know," Rabbit said, sighing again. "He wouldn't anyways. He'd tell the adults."

"You have to give him an excuse to not going hunting with him today," Durril said. "Something he'll believe and not ask too many questions about."

Rabbit nodded. "I'll take care of it."

She walked back to the pod. Durril and Alafair followed but stayed in the shadows. Wyatt was lacing up his own boots now. He gave her a gap-toothed grin when she came in.

"Ready to go?" he asked.

"I can't today."

Wyatt stood up and raised an eyebrow at her. "Why not? You sick? I can take you to the infirmary."

"No, I'm not sick. I got my first woman's bleeding today."

Wyatt's face turned a bright red. "Oh... yeah, um, no problem, Rabbit. Rest up then. Or whatever."

He hurried to collect his spear and bow and made a fast exit out the tunnel.

Alafair grinned.

"Don't ever think of using that excuse with me," Durril said quietly.

Alafair held a hand to her chest. "Who? Me? I would never..."

Rabbit got her own spear and bow and returned to Durril and Alafair.

"We have to leave through your hatch," she said. "It's the farthest out. No one will see us."

The three made their way back to Durril and Alafair's pod and then up to the surface. The sky was nearly all cloud again, and a thick grey fog hovered a few feet above the ground. It wouldn't wear off until midday, and not at all if the sun didn't put in an appearance.

Alafair took a few steps away from Durril and Rabbit, the fog causing her outline to blur. She could only see about a meter past her nose.

"Well, where do we go?" she asked, hands on hips.

"North," Rabbit said.

"You're sure?" Durril asked.

Alafair didn't wait for confirmation but started walking north through the fog. Durril hurried to catch up with her, making sure she didn't get out of sight.

"You're pretty brave for a garbage collector," Rabbit said to Durril after they were a mile or so away from the Ant Hills, too far to run into anyone or to be overheard by warriors.

"Thanks," Durril replied. The compliment

was back-handed, but it was the best you could expect from a warrior. Uncle Papin said they thought they were above everyone else. To Durril, it seemed like everyone thought their job was the most important to the colony, but really, none of them would get by alone. Everyone had to make peace with whatever their job was, even if it was as unglamorous as digging debris from the dirt.

"What if we don't find anything?" Rabbit asked, quietly. Alafair was out of earshot, increasing her distance ahead of them as the fog started to burn off.

Durril shrugged. "Then we just go back I guess."

"And what if we do find something?"

"Then we find out what it is and what happened to Uncle Papin."

Rabbit didn't respond for a moment as she made a trail in the dirt beside her with the tip of her bow. "Do you think it's them?"

"Them who?"

She let out an exasperated sigh and hoisted her bow back over her shoulder. "You know. Them. The ones who brought us here. The Angels."

"You mean the aliens."

Rabbit rolled her eyes. "Whatever they are, they're what took us from Earth a long, long time ago and now we're here. Do you think they've come back?"

"How am I supposed to know? I wasn't there. No one was there, no one who's alive anymore."

They both lapsed into silence, and the fog completely wore off in the sun now smoldering above them. Durril looked back the way they had come. A light breeze had covered their footprints, and the Ant Hills were well beyond their view now. All that lay behind them was the grey expanse of nothingness that stopped at the horizon.

"They called Earth the blue planet," Rabbit said. "Just like the stones we sometimes find here. Can you imagine anything alive that could be that blue, Durril?"

He tried to imagine it, but it looked all wrong; just his own world with dull blue dust. Nothing special.

"Durril! I found it!" Alafair came running back to them to tug on Durril's sleeve. "It's real big."

Durril and Rabbit followed Alafair to the crest of a shallow hill, until they saw it too. The three children crouched to peek over the hill and down at the oblong metal craft.

"It's bigger than one of our pods," Alafair said.

"It's like four of our pods," Rabbit said as she notched an arrow in her bow.

"Let's go see if anyone's inside," Durril said, standing up and starting towards it.

"What?!" Rabbit hissed, grabbing his shirt and hauling him back down. "You don't know what's in there."

"Uncle Papin is in there. If we found it, then so did he."

"We should go back and get help," Rabbit said.

"They won't come. You know how afraid they are of even wandering a couple meters away from the colony. The only people allowed are warriors and scavengers. That's us, Rabbit."

She bit her lip and looked back at the craft. Its metal shell shone in the midmorning sunlight like a strange, chrome gemstone.

Durril had his own doubts despite his brave speech. It was the job of scavengers and warriors to go beyond the area that was deemed safe by the colony, but not until they were older, and had completed multiple chaperoned missions.

"Fine," Rabbit agreed. "But I go first."

Durril nodded his assent and took Alafair by the hand. It was decided, no turning back.

"I don't need a babysitter," Alafair protested.

"Shh, Alafair. This isn't a game." Durril pulled her scarf up over her head. "If there's trouble, you run, okay?"

"But--"

Durril took her face between his hands and looked into her grey eyes. "You have to promise me. I let you bring your knife, so you owe me, okay?"

Alafair extended her pinkie finger towards him. "Pinkie promise."

Durril wrapped his own little finger around hers. "Pinkie promise."

Durril and Alafair followed Rabbit closer to the ship. It was smooth, with no windows or entrances. It had no seams to show where it had been put together, as if it had been sculpted from a single piece of metal. Three tripod legs with circular disks at the ends held it up above the dirt, keeping its belly clean and shining.

Rabbit approached the craft but did not touch it. She started circling it, her bow raised until she got to the other side and found an entrance. It was an arching rectangular void, too dark inside to see anything. No steps led down from it, but someone had come outside and walked around, leaving prints in the dirt far larger than their own. Long narrow boot treads marked the ground a few stops from the craft, and then turned around and walked back, up into the hollow darkness. Someone just getting some air.

"Help me up," Rabbit whispered to Durril, tucking her bow under her arm. "I'll check it out and pull you up after."

Durril grabbed her waist and tried his best to hoist her up to the opening, though she managed most of it on her own by pulling herself up with her free hand. The moment she was on her feet again, her arrow was notched and pointed ahead.

"Stay here," she said, then disappeared into the void.

Alafair grabbed Durril's hand, squeezing it tight. "Don't leave me out here," she whispered.

Durril squeezed back. "I won't."

She was looking up into the opening, waiting for Rabbit to reappear and biting her lip in anticipation. Durril lifted her into his arms, and for once she didn't protest.

The wind had picked up, covering the odd footprints and forming tiny dunes around the circular feet of the craft. Alafair buried her face in Durril's shoulder to keep the dust out of her eyes. The sun was only just coming to its peak, but they would have to head back within an hour or risk being caught out at night.

Rabbit returned, bow lowered, and waved them up. Durril let out the breath he had been holding and lifted Alafair up first. Rabbit pulled him up after with much more ease than when he had lifted her.

Silently, she motioned for the two of them to follow, and Alafair and Durril did, holding hands. They were in a narrow hallway that felt like a metal tunnel, cold and unnatural. Soon the light outside faded, and the glow of little green orbs hung from the ceiling by thin metal cables dimly illuminated their path. The hall soon opened up into a larger room, lit with larger orbs and smaller lights in the floor that ran parallel to the walls. There were apparitions around the sides of the room—maps and charts with letters Durril didn't understand. They were all the pale green of the lights, and they floated transparent above the floor with no visible tethering.

These held his attention only momentarily, because Uncle Papin lay naked on a silver table in the center of the room. Wires stuck his flesh on all sides, and little clear circles were suctioned to his ribs, chest, and forehead.

Durril looked to Rabbit for permission to move closer, nervous. She nodded and he went to his Uncle, Alafair close behind him. Rabbit backed into the room, her bow aimed at the entrance. It seemed to be the only way in or out.

Alafair was too short to see her Uncle well, even straining on her tip-toes, little fingers grasping the table ledge just above her upturned nose. Durril stood at eye level with him. His skin was wet with perspiration, his brown hair damp and sticking to his forehead. Durril watched his chest move up and down, and his breath rustled the hairs of his thick mustache.

"Is he dead?" Alafair whispered.

Durril shook his head.

Alafair wandered over to one of the green screens that was low enough for her to touch the bottom of. Her hand went right through it, her fingers awash with a pale green tint.

Black symbols appeared on her hand and arm, distorted and elongated against her skin.

Durril thought he heard a sound coming from one of the screens, or maybe the ceiling above him. He looked up at the metal ceiling, slightly domed, arching from one wall to the other. It was a whistling sound, like air leaking out of a hole in a tire, but it wasn't coming from above him.

Alafair shrieked and ran for Durril, taking her knife from her belt even as she took refuge behind him. Rabbit and Durril turned to the entrance in unison and Rabbit gasped before raising her bow and burying an arrow into the chest of a green figure outlined against the dark hallway behind it.

It was tall, easily a head taller than the tallest man in the colony, and its arms hung awkwardly beside its lanky torso—two of them at least. Another pair of arms, protruding just below the other two, held a silver cup, nursing it with all eight of its fingers.

Grey tube-like appendages were aligned in rows along the top of its scalp, all pulled to the back of its head, and as Durril stared wide-eyed at its face—milky blue eyes, tiny nose barely disturbing the smooth curves of its cheeks, large nearly transparent lips—he realized it's skin was pure white. Its textureless surface only appeared green because of the lights in the hallway, which seemed attracted to it like mechanical moths.

Rabbit already had another arrow notched when the silver cup hit the floor with a clatter, metal against metal. The alien dropped to its knees, staring down at the arrow in its breast, its four arms hovering inactive beside it as if it had forgotten it had any at all. A slim line of pink pus began leaking from the wound, spilling over the grey mesh it wore as a covering. It made a wheezing sound, stretched its two left hands out to Durril, and then toppled over onto its right side, legs folding awkwardly beneath it.

The room was silent. Durril could feel Alafair quivering against his hip, and Rabbit's bow shook uncontrollably in her hands.

"Did you kill it?" Alafair asked quietly.

Rabbit lowered her bow. "I don't know."

Durril approached the fallen alien and Rabbit raised her bow again, aiming at its head. Durril got closer, and noticed its breath hissing through its lips. The broad chest heaved, tugging hard to get air in. Its eyes were closed, long black eyelashes lying against its white skin.

"I think it's a girl," Alafair whispered, coming closer to the creature while still making sure Durril was between her and it.

"Me too," Durril said noticing small breasts restrained behind the mesh suit. The coils on its head had been braided similarly to Rabbit's hair, except in a single braid with each coil distinctly separate, not blending as hair would.

"But what is it?" Rabbit asked, lowering her bow when she realized that the alien wasn't getting up.

"I don't know," Durril said, crouching beside it. "Is it the only one on board, do you think?"

Rabbit shook her head. "I walked around the whole ship. It's all one big open space except for the tunnel, this room, and one other--but it was empty. There must be a room I didn't find."

"Take Alafair and go see. I don't want anyone else sneaking up on us."

"I can't just leave you here alone," Rabbit said.

"I'll be fine. I need to get her sitting up, maybe we can help her."

"Help her?" Alafair asked accusingly.

"Well we don't know if she meant us any harm. Maybe she's friendly and we just shot her."

Rabbit knotted her brow, troubled.

Alafair crossed her arms over her chest. "Uncle Papin is naked on some dissection table. I don't think she's friendly, Durril."

"Alafair, just go with Rabbit. Now."

She rolled her eyes at him but followed as Rabbit left the room, scanning the hallway again for movement before moving on.

Durril grabbed the alien under her lower set of arms and dragged her to the nearest wall, propping her up so her back was resting against it, her pointed chin hanging onto her chest.

Durril left her there and went back to Uncle Papin. He inspected the various wires dug into his veins; he could see the needles shallowly embedded under his skin. Durril wondered if anything attached to him would help her, but thought better of trying anything alone. His knowledge of anatomy consisted of one occasion when he had watched Rabbit skin a lox, and he had lost his dinner.

Rabbit and Alafair returned then to report that they had indeed found a third room.

"It's a pilot's chamber of some sort with a big window, which is weird, because I didn't see a window from the outside," Rabbit said.

"It must be invisible," Alafair added.

"There was no one else on the ship?" Durril asked.

"Not that we found. And there's only the one bed in that other room so I guess it's alone." Rabbit slipped her bow over her torso, sandwiching herself between the body and string so it crossed diagonally over her chest. Then she removed the scarf around her neck and laid it across Papin's waist, covering his genitals.

"Thought the man deserved some dignity," she muttered, more to herself than the other two children.

"Can we use anything here to help her?" Durril asked.

Rabbit shrugged, looking down at the wires. "Maybe this." She took a needle from a vein in his left wrist.

She stood there holding it for a moment as she watched to see if Uncle Papin's state changed. When she was confident that his condition was stable she moved with her wire over to the alien.

"Umm, which arm?" she asked.

Durril shrugged.

Rabbit chose the lower one which was laying limp on the floor beside her, palm up. It had no effect.

"What about the circles?" Durril asked.

Rabbit went back to Uncle Papin and selected two of the clear circles from his chest, peeling them off with her fingernail. Again, there was no change in his condition. She crouched beside the alien once again and pressed the circles against the alien's chest. They stuck. Her wheezing breath steadied, and her eyes fluttered open.

She looked at the children with confusion, then down at the arrow in her chest.

"Are you alright?" Alafair asked, regaining her usual confidence and stepping closer to her, even crouching down beside her as Rabbit did.

The alien blinked her big round eyes and lifted her wrist in front of her to examine the needle. She felt around on her chest with another hand until she found the adhesive circles. Then she returned her hands to her sides and let out a noise that Durril thought sounded like gargling water.

The three stared back at her in confusion.

She pointed past them to the table Uncle Papin was on.

"He's alright," Durril said.

She pointed again, jabbing the air with her white finger.

Durril looked once more and noticed a small round disk sitting on the edge of the table above Uncle Papin's left shoulder. He retrieved it and brought it back to the alien.

"What if it's a weapon?" Rabbit hissed.

Durril hesitated.

"She's a giant, Rabbit," Alafair said. "If she wanted to hurt us she could have strangled us by now, even with that arrow in her."

Rabbit still looked skeptical, but Durril made up his mind and passed the disk to the alien. She accepted it and placed the tiny disk near her throat, at the hollow center of her collar bone.

She opened her mouth again: "Little humans."

The children jumped back in surprise. She

seemed to clear her throat, as if adjusting to the unnatural voice.

"You should not be here. Why have you come and why have you injured me so?" The words were monotone and quiet. Durril wondered if the disk was capable of expressing her tone or emotion.

"It was an accident," Rabbit said, quickly. "I was scared you'd hurt us."

The alien looked down at her wrist again then back at Rabbit.

"You have helped me."

Rabbit nodded. "We were just guessing, really."

"What are you doing to Uncle Papin?" Durril jumped in.

"The man?" The alien asked, nodding to the table.

"Yes, him."

"Check-up. Testing for virus."

"What virus?"

She shook her head, causing her braid to fall over her shoulder. "You will not know."

They fell silent. Durril wanted to demand answers, but he didn't want to make her mad.

"What's your name?" Alafair asked.

"Tu," The alien replied.

"That's a dumb name."

"Alafair!"

Tu made a clicking sound in her throat which Durril interpreted as laughter judging by the slight rising and falling of her shoulders and the thin lines that appeared around her nose and eyes. The laugh was immediately followed by a cough and she shut her eyes again.

"Can we do anything to help?" Durril asked.

The alien nodded but took a few deep breaths before opening her eyes again.

"Help me get to my cockpit. It will not take me long to get back to Base. They can heal me there."

Rabbit and Durril stood on either side of her and helped her to her feet. She was too tall to put her arms around their necks but took support from putting her hands on their shoulders instead. Rabbit and Durril each had an arm around her waist to keep her from falling backwards.

Alafair walked ahead of them. "So this thing can fly?"

"Yes," Tu responded.

"Alafair, don't ask her questions, she's having a hard enough time just walking," Durril said.

"It's alright," Tu said, patting his head with one of her hands. "I am not dying. My body is more resilient than yours."

"What's going to happen to Uncle Papin?" Rabbit asked.

Tu did not answer. She closed her eyes again and tipped her head forward as they walked. Durril and Rabbit exchanged a worried look, but continued the walk to the cockpit in silence. Arriving in the small room that had originally escaped Rabbit's notice, they helped Tu into a reclined S-back chair facing the large window.

Spanning half of the room, from the floor to the roof and the curved wall in between, the window made the nose of the ship into a bubble-like observatory. Durril imagined what it would look like while flying in space, surrounded by the black cape of the galaxy, carefully placed stars sewn into its fabric.

Tu swiveled in her chair to face them, back to the darkening desert outside her cockpit. "Your Uncle has a virus. Him and many others in your colony. Due to our genetic interferences, we have managed to give your generation immunity. A huge success."

"Who are 'we'? What interferences are you talking about?" Durril asked.

"My people saved your people from Earth hundreds of years ago. I believe you have built that into your mythology?"

"The Angels?" Rabbit asked. "They took us from earth and brought us to a paradise to start over."

"This is no paradise," Durril said.

"No, it is not," Tu said. "It was our goal to remove you from Earth because it was dying and you did not yet have the means to leave on your own. It was deemed a waste of life—how selfish would we have been, to know of your plight but leave you to your fate unaided. We are a nomadic people with no planet to call home ourselves, so finding a planet for you was a difficult task. We split you up, sent you to planets that had the most to offer but could only support smaller societies."

"There are other people?" Alafair asked. "On other planets?"

Tu nodded. "Most didn't make it. We didn't have a lot of time, and some of our calculations were incorrect. We also made rash assumptions about your kind before we understood you. You do not behave as we do. Some colonies were unadaptable to their planets, some warred amongst themselves, and others gave up. It was decidedly too risky to interfere more than we already had."

"But you did interfere with us," Durril said.

"Yes. You were one of the most successful colonies from the beginning, and when we saw there was a threat to your survival, we stepped in. There is a natural virus on this planet that seems to be hostile to parasites, which is what it considers you. It's been trying to wipe you out, and it has been winning the fight, until now."

"Is it going to kill Uncle Papin?" Alafair asked.

"No," Tu said. She sighed and reached down to a metal compartment beside her chair, feeling around for something inside.

"What I am about to tell you may upset you, but I would ask that you try and think about your species, not just your family. I know I am asking a lot from such young minds."

She removed a gun from the compartment and set it in her lap. It was white and plastic and all round edges. It looked like a toy. The colony didn't have guns, but that was no accident. They lacked the materials for them to be practical but there was also an unspoken law, a flavor from a past life that had evidently left a bad taste in the mouths of their founders. Stories were still told, pictures drawn—with all the tragedy and devastation of such morality tales.

Rabbit's indrawn breath told Durril that she recognized the weapon too. Alafair seemed un-phased by its appearance, but Durril caught her take note of her distance from the door with a flicker of her eyes.

"We can handle it," Durril said.

Tu bit her bottom lip with her front teeth, just as Rabbit often did when nervous or indecisive, showing off pointed incisors.

"The virus turns the host into a mindless predator," she explained. "It becomes a tool for the planet, another defense mechanism rather than an intelligent life form using up its resources. Those who already have the virus must be exterminated before they can become such tools, or else they will cripple your chances of survival."

"You mean over half our colony has to die?" Rabbit said, voice wavering over the words.

"It will be a damaging loss, yes, and put your productivity and advancement back a few years. You will survive it."

"What happened to those who have had the virus in the past?" Durril said. "Did you kill them too?"

"Some we exterminated without the knowledge of the colony. Many never contracted the virus to begin with. Those who did, the ones we didn't catch in time, were taken by the planet."

"The things that hunt the Moaners," Alafair said.

"Yes," Tu confirmed.

Durril could feel the color drain from his face.

"Those are humans?" Rabbit asked.

"Those were humans," Tu corrected.

"And everyone else in the colony is going to turn into those things?" Durril asked.

"How did we not know?" Rabbit interrupted. "How could people turn into those monsters without us noticing?"

"We took care of it. If the colony had panicked, chances of survival would have plummeted." Tu turned to Durril, meeting his eyes. "Those infected have to be killed. A worse fate awaits them otherwise."

"So you've come alone to kill hundreds of people?" Durril asked. His initial fear at the revelation had passed and anger was taking its place. Why did these aliens think they had the right to keep such things from them all this time?

"We've created a poison for your water

supply. It won't harm your generation or any others that managed to avoid infection."

Rabbit stared out the cockpit window. Tears began running down her cheeks and leaving streaks in the dust that had found its way to her face despite her scarf. She sniffled and looked like she might really start to cry. Alafair stared up at her, eyes glistening, and took her hand. Tears were a contagious thing.

Durril wanted to send Tu away, to curse her for all she had told them and for all she had kept from them.

"We'll do it," Rabbit said, chocking back a sob.

"Rabbit?" Durril said, it was half a question, half an accusation.

"What will happen when half our colony becomes those things, Durril? We can't fight them."

"So you want to murder them all now, when they don't suspect it?" Durril said, raising his voice.

Rabbit crossed her arms over her chest. Her eyes were still spilling over, but her glare was determined. "Would you rather die, or become one of those things?"

Durril's hands balled up into fists at his sides which he couldn't loosen. Furiously, he wiped his face with his sleeve, leaving marks of dirt behind like war paint. He found his cheeks were just as wet as Rabbit's.

"That is not our decision," Durril said.

"Yes it is," Tu said. She let her gun rest in her lap and held her hand out to them, palm up, revealing the second item she had removed from the compartment. A small blue vial.

"Perhaps it's time we let you decide your own fate, little humans," Tu said. "This colony will be in your hands either way."

Momma's back gleamed in the sunlight as she used her attachable spade to flatten the soil around the base of the pink flowers she had just planted: a gift from Tu upon Alafair's request for colour.

Each grave was marked with such a plant. They were impractical, produced no fruit or medicinal property but practicality had been the colonies sole focus for too long and Durril was adamant that more real living be done – if such a thing were possible in the face of so much death.

The colony had gone from a population of 2000 to 854 overnight. They died in their sleep which had left the remaining colonists with an unpleasant awakening and a long day of digging. Three weeks later, Tu had returned as promised with the color and new life they had so desperately needed.

What Durril, Alafair, and Rabbit had learned in Tu's ship had stayed there. The deaths had been attributed to an unknown disease of epidemic proportions, and were being considered as the greatest loss in the history of the colony. For a while there was fear that the disease would wipe them out completely, but after a month had passed without other deaths, it was considered over. The graves were marked, and the matter was put to rest with the dead.

Tu's return had also remained a secret to the colony, but Durril had sent her away with a proposition to her people: make contact with our colony. The history wouldn't need to be discussed, but he suggested that they identify themselves as a nomadic people with an interest in the colony. It wouldn't necessarily be a lie, and proposing friendship would provide a legitimate, honest way to interact in the future, even letting the colony ask for help if it needed it.

She had yet to return, but had warned them it might be a long time before she did. Durril wondered what that meant. Tu knew what three weeks had meant, but long and short time spans were relative. Tu had seen the death of Earth, so her lifetime must be very long indeed, nearly infinite to Durril's own.

Durril watched the grey soil grow dark and damp as Alafair followed Momma along the rows of flowers with her watering can. Her necklace of blue stones looked more natural with the bright petals of the plants (she had told Aunt Beti she found them on a scavenging mission). She had given a similar blue necklace to Tu, and had radiated with pride when Tu had accepted and immediately hung it around her neck, happy to take the gift back to her people.

Durril jumped as he felt the butt of a spear poke him between his shoulder blades. Rabbit was back from her morning scouting mission. She still had Wyatt for a scouting partner, but every few nights after midnight, she and Durril shared a secret task. On such missions, they put use to the second gift Tu had given them: her gun. They went out, armed with flashlights and the gun between them, and eliminated the used-to-be humans one by one. The creatures were mutated beyond recognition, and they haunted the few hours of sleep Durril stole each night, but they also reminded him that they had made the right decision.

"Find anything interesting today, garbage boy?" Rabbit asked, prodding his back again with her spear before flipping it right end up.

"A boomerang," Durril said.

Rabbit laughed. "A what?"

Durril took the curved wooden toy from his belt and showed it to her. "It must have come from Earth with the original colonists, and gotten lost. I found it buried in the dirt."

"What's it do?"

"You throw it and then it comes back to you."

"No way."

Durril turned towards the horizon, the sun a heavy drop of golden dew, not a cloud in sight. The hatches to the Ant Hills were all sitting open to let some fresh air in, and fans were blowing down below to increase circulation.

Durril aimed towards the farthest hatch, his own, and let the boomerang fly over the grey desert towards it. He watched it spin round and round over the earth until it was a speck in the distance, an irrelevant object caught up in an unstoppable rotation with a trajectory all its own.

"I'd like to meet them," Durril said.

"Who?" Rabbit asked squinting into the sun.

"The other humans on other planets."

She looked at him. "We can't even get off our own."

"Tu can. Maybe she'd take me with her."

"Big dreams for a garbage boy."

Durril shook his head. "There's more than this out there, Rabbit."

"Leaving this planet to find other colonies. Going back to Earth. Do you think any of it's really possible?"

A little dark shadow came into view before them across the grey sands. As it spun closer and closer to them Durril planted his feet where he thought it would pass. He caught the toy with ease, the rough grain putting splinters in his fingers.

He smiled. "I do."

PRIOTER 7

White and blue meet at the horizon. There's nothing but tundra for miles. I make sure to stand far enough away from the heard of Rhaapiti gathered close by while still keeping an eye on my partner as she makes her gradual approach toward them across the snow. She walks with her revolver in one hand and her scythe strapped to her back to free up her other.

"How are they looking, Arly?" I ask her through the microphone attached to the inside of my fishbowl helmet.

"Lookin' good, Raeyan." She responds. "Pegasus and Appletini are on duty as always. It looks like everyone has eaten and are in a state of blissful digestion. Join me?"

I start slowly making my way across the snow. The Rhaapiti are huge orange beasts that look like a cross between an elk and a rhinoceros and they do not like to be startled. The impressive gray antlers possessed by the males of the species are used for fighting and defense and the one giant horn on their nose, a feature of both sexes, is used for digging up their favorite snacks: blizzard root. They come to approximately seven feet not including their antlers.

The alpha male of the heard, who I had named Pegasus, stands watching the horizon as his family lay down to relax after eating their full. He is accompanied by his mate and alpha female who Arly had so cheekily named after her favorite cocktail.

"Hey there boy, how are ya?" I speak quietly through my helmet as I come up beside Pegasus. He snorts but shows no hostility as I lay my hand against his rough skin, rubbing my palm over the pours in his orange hide. They let out a toxic gas if frightened or angered which would kill me or Arly in seconds if exposed, not to mention the whole atmosphere was polluted with a similar gas. We had to wear ultra-organized latex particle suits that covered our whole bodies, including every individual finger and toe, right up until the skin-tight fabric met our helmets at the base of our necks.

Taking my own revolver from the belt around my waist I stick the barrel between Pegasus' neck and shoulder joint, the only inch of flesh that can be easily penetrated.

"Just a pinch now," I whisper.

I hear the click of the first syringe snapping out and then wait the eight seconds it takes to click back in. The cylinder spins, lining up the next chamber, and I pull the trigger again. Four more times and then it's full.

"Good boy Pegasus." I pat his shoulder and look around for Arly. She's beside Appletini, emptying her full syringes into the pouch on her belt. I do the same and the two of us move on to other Rhaapiti, walking calming amid the docile creatures. The alphas won't let us approach the heard until we say our hellos to them so they can sniff us out and make sure we aren't a threat.

The job is dangerous and the cold climate harsh and unforgiving but it serves a valuable purpose to the Inter Planet Military, our employers. They are in charge of our solar systems defenses and part of that is having a technically advanced military. Rhaapiti blood can be frozen in to a solid and then smelted in the strongest substance available in the entire galaxy. 'Indestructible' they're calling it and they're coating every single military craft in it. A big, expensive undertaking for peacetime. A lot of people are asking questions. I'm not one of them. I just do my job.

Me and Arly finish collecting our blood samples from all forty-eight Rhaapiti, a task that takes nearly all morning, and then we jump on our Solarboards and head back to base.

Sapron Hollow base camp is located in Crater B giving us a total of 57, 600 square feet to temporarily call home. Of course the network of buildings that makes up Sapron Hallow is only a small portion of that and our living quarters a smaller portion still. The rest is dedicated to the labs, medical wing, and the cargo hold. Missions at Sapron Hollow could last anywhere from three weeks to eight months — the longest amount of time dubbed safe to be exposed, even with all our safety gear, to the toxic atmosphere.

For collectors like me and Arly that number is dropped to a max of five months because we come into direct contact with the Rhaapiti who are practically a moving toxic storm cloud.

Sapron Hollow is on Prioter 7. Being so far away from our sun it can get pretty cold. Our suits are insulated well but we are both still eager for some warm clothes once we get back to base. We leave our Solarboards laying on the snow to soak up the rays and charge, and head in to the detox chamber. We strip down and turn on the shower which sprays us from all directions with high pressured water and whatever else the contamination team felt was necessary to blast our bodies with. I try not to think about the chemical bath I receive daily.

Once we are dry and clothed Arly embraces me in a spontaneous hug. I laugh in surprise and hug her back.

"I'm going to miss you," She says into my shoulder. She is a head shorter than me and I get a face full of her blond curls.

"Aww I'll miss you too, Arly."

"I wish I didn't have to go."

"Arly," I hold her out at arm's length. "You have a husband waiting for you back on Acroniatera. Not to mention you are having a baby and you do not want to do that on this snowball. Do you hear me?"

Arly laughs and places her palm against her tummy which doesn't yet show signs of the life within. "Your right. But I'll miss you too much."

"I'll be back home before you pop that baby out."

She sighs and recomposes herself. "Alright then, let's go meet my replacement."

"I don't think anyone could replace you."

She fans her face with her hand. "Stop it, you're gonna make me cry."

"Okay, okay, let's go."

Arly's pregnancy was sending her home early; they didn't want the baby being exposed to the same stuff they had no problem exposing grown women too. So they had to send in a replacement for her or else it would take me twice as long to collect the blood samples, and here on Prioter 7 everything is about efficiency.

The new recruits are always briefed in the labs so that's where we head. We find Dr. Brod — Arly calls him Dr. Bod because of his trim figure — lecturing a young man on Rhaapiti anatomy. He is quite animated as he always is when discussing his work but more surprising is that the young man seems entirely captivated by the discussion.

"Poor sucker," Arly says. "Looks like the Doctor's stuck on tangent mode again."

"The kid doesn't look like he minds."

Arly shrugs. "If he can listen to this scientific dribble then all the power to him."

Dr. Brod catches sight of us and stops mid-sentence. "Ah Arly, Raeyan, come in, come in."

The recruit looks almost human, except for the pointed ears and the faint green tint to his skin. He bows slightly at Arly and then at me, causing his black hair to fall across his brow.

"Nice to meet you." I stick out my hand. "I'm Raeyan."

He looks at my hand awkwardly for a moment.

"The girls are from Acroniatera and shaking hands is considered a greeting there," the doctor says.

"Oh." He smiles and grabs my hand awkwardly. His grip is strange and I notice he has six fingers instead of five and all are the exact same length minus the thumb which is only slightly longer than my own.

"I'm Teag, from Polyphemus."

"What is Polyphemus?"

"It's what the natives call Prioter 4," Dr. Brod clarifies.

"Why?" Arly asks.

"It has a big sand storm in the Tectonic Desert which never stops and it looks like a giant eye from space."

Arly stares at him blankly.

"This is Arly," I say, interjecting. "She'll be training you until she leaves and then you will replace her full time."

"Nice to meet you," he says, holding out his hand just as I had. Arly shakes it, making a face when she feels his odd fingers. He doesn't appear to notice.

"So how did you end up getting sent here? Usually they send young guys like you to the mines on Prioter 2," Arly asks.

"I volunteered," Teag responds.

Me and Arly share a skeptical look.

"I'm a zoologist student at the Academy and the Rhaapiti are a very interesting species to me, but since they can't survive off planet the only way to study them was to come to them."

"Whoa, whoa hold up," Arly says, waving her hands at him. "You're from the Academy? You're not IPM? You've had no military training? No outer planet evac drills or exotic survival courses?"

Teag enthusiastically shakes his head no.

"Are you nuts?"

"Arly!"

"What?" she crosses her arms over her chest. "If we get invaded or there's an asteroid collision, he's doomed."

Teag doesn't look worried. He brushes his hair back onto his head as he looks around at the various photographs and Rhaapiti diagrams Dr. Brod has put up around the lab.

"Well it's a good thing neither of those things are likely to happen," I say.

"Famous last words," Arly shoots back.

I stick my tongue out at her. She responds likewise.

"I want Teag out in the field tomorrow with you girls so make sure he is at least briefed on the scythe tonight," Dr. Brod instructs. "Now get to dinner the three of you. You know the cook is merciless with late comers."

Meals are not one of the highlights of life at Sapron Hollow. Very little grows here so we have to ship in most of our food. This is thought of as a pesty expense by those high and mighty so they decided upon a solution: a prototype crop cloning machine. All you have to do is put a vegetable or fruit into the machine and two come out. The problem is it only seems to work with potatoes. Everything else comes out the other end in a big squishy pile of mush – I guess that's why it's a prototype.

Thankfully the cooks are resourceful and they use the perfectly edible mush to make smoothies and pie. And so everyone at Sapron Hollow lives off of watered down smoothies, a vast assortment of pie, and mashed potatoes, backed potatoes, scalloped potatoes, and practically every other way a potato can be cooked. The variety does not make the vegetable any easier to choke down day after day.

"Is there any water?" Teag asks, looking around the cafeteria.

"It's unsafe to drink because of the toxicity. Even after purifying it multiple times it killed the mice in about three seconds," I tell him.

He cringes, looking down at his dry french-fries. "Ketchup?"

I shake my head. "We each get rations of water. You'll find some in your room when you go back. We get a little more than everyone else because of the demands of our job but I recommend saving it. You'll be really thirsty when you get back tomorrow."

Arly joins us, juggling three plates as she sits down.

"What is it today?" I ask.

"Blueberry, pumpkin, and rhubarb." Arly says, pointing to each plate of pie in turn.

"You just eat pie?" Teag asks her.

"I hate french-fries," Arly replies, sticking out her tongue in disgust. "Plus, my baby deserves tasty things."

"Baby?"

"Arly's pregnant. That's why she's being sent home."

"Oh. Congratulations."

"What? On being knocked up? It's not much of an accomplishment. It's not like I ran a marathon or anything."

I nudge Arly with my elbow. "She's kidding. She is very excited to be a mom."

Teag doesn't look convinced.

"What smoothie is it today?" Arly asks.

"Mango." I reply.

She jumps up from her chair and struts off across the cafeteria to fetch one of her own.

"You'll get used to her humor," I tell Teag. "She's a little abrupt but she's like a marsh mellow on the inside."

Teag laughs, pushing his plate of fries away. "If you say so."

We finish our meals and then show Teag the armory. When we finally get him to stop drooling over the life size model of a female Rhaapiti I start the instruction.

"Okay, so this is the suit you'll be wearing."

I give him the new suit and let him feel the material.

"Why does he get a green one?" Arly asks. "Ours are those plain black things. They may be slimming but they are soo boring."

"I don't know, just the new model I guess."

"I'm going to look naked," Teag says, holding the suit up next to his pale green face.

"You'll be okay," Arly says. "It's a few shades darker than you are."

"Can we please get back to the instructions?" I say, hands on hips.

Teag looks at me, expectantly waiting for his lesson. Arly just crosses her arms and sticks her tongue out at me.

"The suit is straight forward: put it on, zip it up, you know how it is. This is the revolver we use to collect the blood." I hand Teag the gun. He accepts it nervously.

"It's not a real gun. You're not going to shoot anything with it," Arly says.

"What you do is put the barrel right here, right by the shoulder." I show him where I mean on the model. "Then you pull the trigger, it will click, and wait until you hear it click again. That means the first syringe is full and you can pull the trigger again. You do this six times in total."

"What if you do it more?"

"Can you count to six?" Arly asks.

Teag nods

"Then you shouldn't have a problem."

"You'll get used to it, Teag." I say

"Now this," Arly removes one of the silver scythes from the wall, holding onto the leather wrapped wooden handle. "Is the most important tool you will have. This is the difference between life and death."

Arly stands beside the Rhaapiti model and holds the scythe in her right hand.

"If the animal gets startled or feels threatened it will charge you. It's not their fault, they aren't aggressive creatures, but it happens. They are only protecting their family from perceived danger, just like you or I would do." Arly brings the tip of the scythe against the models neck, the same place we take blood samples from. "This is the only weak spot on a Rhaapiti's body. If you feel like you're in trouble take the tip and thrust it in between the bones. Don't go too deep or you'll never get it out again. Once it's in about a third of the way rotate it and pull it out. Your going through muscle so pull like your life depends on it, because it will."

Teag looks like he might vomit. "Have you ever had to do it?"

"Only once," Arly admits. "On one of my first runs a bull attacked my trainer. We were really lucky because he was small and we were at the edge of the heard when it happened. If we had been in the middle I don't know if we could have gotten away."

"Was your trainer alright?"

"Yeah he was fine. He had been attached many times before. The heard just doesn't take well to some people."

"What happened to the bull?" Teag asks.

"We went back the next day and brought it to the lab for analysis. The scientists were in their glory."

"Well that's all we can really show you tonight," I say, returning the revolver to its drawer. "Everything else you have to learn can only be taught in the field."

"So get some shut eye kid," Arly says. She returns her scythe and we leave Teag in the armory examining the Rhaapiti.

"I can't breathe." Teag is sitting on his Solarboard, legs hanging over the edge just above the ground. "I think my suit is too tight."

"Come on, Teag." I'm standing in front of him. Mine and Arlys boards are already powered down and laying on the snow, their silvery blue tops almost look like surf board laying a white sandy beach – only the cold breaks the illusion.

Arly is already started in the direction of the heard and I want to be moving too to keep from freezing my backside off. "It will be fine. Me and Arly are professionals and we've got your back," I say, trying to comfort Teag.

"Has he peed his suit yet?" Arly laughs into my ear piece.

"I can hear you too," Teag grumbles.

Arly laughs again. "I know."

Teag takes a deep breath and slides off his board. He has his hair pulled back in a small bun today revealing the shaved sides of his head and his green ears which come to a yellow point. His anxious breath fogs up his fish bowl but dissipates almost instantly due to the small fan that keeps our body temperatures regulated. He powers off his board and follows me towards the heard.

"This is Pegasus." I pat the large Rhaapiti on his flanks. "I named him that because of the markings on his side. The dark spots kind of look like wings, don't you think?"

Teag nods. He stares in awe at the great animal.

"Here, let him smell you."

Teag cups his hands together and brings them up under Pegasus's nose. The animal snorts and rubs his nose against his palms. Teag grins foolishly.

"He likes you," I say. I stick the revolver into his shoulder and start extracting the blood. "You can do the next one."

"They don't mind the needle?" Teag asks.

"Nope. They have thick skin. They barely feel it."

I look out across the plain for Arly. She is already on her third Rhaapiti.

"You're on a roll today, Arly." I say through our mics.

"Yeah."

The simple response and total lack of enthusiasm worries me. I finish with Pegasus and me and Teag move on.

"Is everything okay?" I ask.

There is silence for a moment before she

replies. "The heard seems tense. They have all the babies in the center. Something must be irritating them."

"Maybe Teag just makes them a little nervous. He's someone new." I reply.

"No this is different," Arly insists.

"Do you want to call it?" I ask.

"Yeah, I think we better."

Teag looks at me with worry. "What's wrong?"

"Don't know but Arly thinks we better head back. We'll collect tomorrow."

Teag returns his revolver to his hip and we walk back to our boards.

"Sometimes this happens," I say, in reassurance. "They just get spooked and it's better to let them calm down than risk it."

I look back over my shoulder. Arly is saying goodbye to Appletini at the edge of the heard. She turns away and starts towards us, waving that we shouldn't wait for her.

"They are beautiful creatures," Teag says. "I've seen so many pictures but being right there beside them is so different, surreal."

I find his amazement refreshing. It reminds me of my first run and how in awe I was standing next to the Rhaapiti. I came to Prioter 7 because I needed the job but I fell in love with the animals too.

Teag can't resist another look and throws one last gaze behind us. I stop in my track as I see his eyes widen in fright.

I spin around to see Arly, still a ways behind us, and Appletini trotting after her. Rhaapiti never run unless they feel threatened.

"Arly!" I scream at her through the mic and start running towards her, ripping my scythe off my back. Teag is on my heels. Arly turns when she hears my warning and the Rhaapiti rears up, throwing its massive front hooves up in front of it. Arly hits the snow on her back and I reach her just as the creature puts all its feet back on the ground. It snorts and tries to run at Arly again but I step in front of her, making the beast hesitate.

"Get her on your board!" I yell at Teag. I don't look back to see if he obeys me. I sidestep out of the way of a second flurry of hooves and manage to scoot around beside her. I drive my scythe in between the shoulder and the neck and pull with all my might. She goes down, kneeling on her front legs, then collapsing onto her side. The other Rhaapiti have noticed now and are heading towards me. I throw the bloody scythe into the snow and run towards the boards.

Teag his kneeling beside them with Arly laying out on one next to him. He looks like he's waiting for me.

"Power up the boards, Teag," I pant.

He does and when I get there I run to my board and put it on auto return. It shoots off towards base. I hop on Arly's board, putting a knee on either side of her waist.

"Go!" Teag and I start our boards and soon we are soaring across the tundra. I look down at Arly and to my horror see that her helmet is cracked. There is a massive hole in it above her face and the glass has cut her cheeks and forehead. Her blond curls are splayed out around her head like a halo. Her breath is quiet and quick like distant whistling.

"Arly, I —" I can't speak. She blinks up at me, lips apart. She tries to speak but it comes out as a gasp. She closes her eyes and puts a hand across her belly protectively. I find my voice.

"The baby is going to be okay, Arly. Don't worry. The baby is going to be just fine."

She smiles, as much as she can, and nods. She seems to find comfort in my lie. I speak to her all the way back to base. Talk to her long after her heart stops and her body grows so cold and blue of death has chased the hue from her cheeks.

The boards stop at base, hovering and waiting for me to turn it off. I remove Arly's broken helmet and pushed my own against her forehead, closing my eyes as I cry, my tears trickling onto the glass between us. Teag gets off his board and stands beside us, silent.

I don't remembered getting off the board but somehow I end up in Teag's arms and he is carrying me into the detox chamber. There are people running around us now in their own suits and they are taking Arly away through some other entrance. I try to call out to them, to tell them to stop. That is my friend they are taking away, but sobs shake my body and clog my throat.

Teag puts me down in the detox chamber. He speaks to me, tries to tell me that I have to get clean but I'm paralyzed. His cheeks grow red, an odd addition to his green completion, and then he undoes the zipper on my suit and manages, with patient prompting, to get me to step out of it.

Naked and cold and shell shocked we both endure the proceeding bombardment of water. The bath forces us to close our eyes and there is no chance of talking unless we want to end up with a mouth full of sudsy water. Besides, it is so loud all I can hear is the water rushing past my ears and in them.

I don't know who handed me a towel but I'm wrapped up in one, huddled on the cold tiles of the drying area. I sit like this, entirely alone for a long time until the doors slide open again and Teag comes to sit beside me. He's dressed now and his jeans are getting wet from the puddle that encircles me but he takes no notice.

"Raeyan, Arly is in the export room if you'd like to see her," Teag says quietly. I can see that his hands, which he holds wrapped around his knees, are still shaking.

I nod and he leaves again so I can dress. I want him to come back the minute the doors shut. Suddenly I am through with being alone and crave company. I dress quickly and make my way to the export room. Teag and Dr. Brod are both there standing over Arly laid out on a silver table used to examine plant life and other biological matter the scientist find on the planet – dead things. She doesn't have her suit on anymore. She is wrapped in a white cloth like some Greek priestess, her lean arms lying bare at her sides.

Teag looks uncomfortable, like he doesn't know if he should stay for the intimate farewell of a girl he has only just met. But he does stay and I'm glad for it. He is my partner now after all and besides that I figure he won't mind me crying on his shoulder – well, he might mind but he probably won't say anything.

Dr. Brod will be horribly stiff and clinical about the whole thing. Public displays of emotion make him nervous. He has emotions I'm sure but they are locked somewhere deep inside his rationally wired brain.

"I'm going to put her in a pod which will keep her hygienically frozen. Then we will send her back to Acroniatere with the next shipment of Rhaapiti samples," Dr. Brod explains to me.

I stand beside Teag, looking down at Arly's pretty features, trying to ignore the smattering of cuts that are mixing with her freckles. I grab Teag's hand as Dr. Brod puts restraints around Arlys limbs and torso and one across her forehead to make sure she won't slide around too much during the trip home. Then he wheels her over to the fore mentioned pod and slides the end of the table in to it. He holds up the other end as he folds up the four legs and then slides Arly, table and all, headfirst into the pod, shutting the circular hatch after her.

He looks back at me. I'm still holding on to Teag like he's a life preserver and I'm afraid of drowning in the tears welling up in my eyes. He takes off his glasses and rubs his eyes, sighing. Then he replaces them and speaks as he always does when the conversation isn't about scientific pursuits; in a dry drawl you might expect from one of the old western films they sometimes show in the outdoor theaters.

"Listen, Raeyan, don't be too upset about this. These things happen — the cycle of life and all — and Arly is in better hands now, you know?"

I nod. I did not know but the gesture satisfies him and he leaves the room.

The cold bites harder without Arly's sassy monologue in my ear to keep my mind off my freezing limbs. The suits are insulated and heat regulated but there is only so much to be done against -90 degrees Celsius. -92.3 to be exact. One of the coldest days I've faced yet. I stand beside my hovering board, gripping my shoulders in a bear hug as I wait for Teag to join me.

It's his third week out and he is becoming accustomed to the work but he hasn't yet acquired a liking for the early mornings. It has become habit for me to seek out his room after I shower and pound on his door until he answerers it, boxer clad and blurry eyed, hair mussed from sleep. Then I saunter back to the cafeteria and wait until he joins me to scarf down breakfast and a startling eight cups of strong black tea. Apparently whatever species he is are capable of ingesting much higher amounts of caffeine than humans. I haven't specifically asked Teag what he is. Mostly because I haven't met many aliens (which isn't considered a politically correct term) and I don't know if my nosiness would offend him.

Though the more I get to know him the more I realized there is little that could offend Teag. He comes to breakfast always in a t-shirt and a pair of sweat pants that hang off his too long legs. The overly lanky limbs have a way of tangling with mine under the table as we sit across from each other or tripping me up when I try to pass him, his legs strewn out in front of him as he reclines on the couch in the recreation room. He swears he isn't so clumsy back on his home planet because the furniture is all designed for his extra height but I can't help but imagine a world full of lanky men and women constantly falling over each other who all developed chronic back pain at the age of thirty-five.

After breakfast Teag wanders off to shave in order to keep his bristly black beard off his normally clean cheeks. Then I dress in my suit, power up my board and wait out in the cold. Being alone with the cold each morning has become my time of reflection. I can be as distant as I want, staring off across the tundra, and don't need to worry about Teag asking me if I'm okay, if I need a cup of tea, or Dr. Brod offering me some sort of medication to keep my "dark moods" at bay. I'm not depressed and I hate tea.

Maybe I was a little depressed at first, my best friend just died after all, but after a week back in the field and my mind occupied with training Teag, I was doing better. Then the message came from Fil, Arly's husband, and nearly broke my heart all over again. He was sad, obviously, but wanted to know that I was okay and that if I needed anything I could talk to him. I don't know him all that well, we had only meet on a few occasions, but here he was asking me if I was okay when he was the one who just lost his wife and unborn baby. My mind could not tolerate the selflessness and unfairness of it all and I cried for a good hour until my body stopped producing tears and then just continued shaking with sobs and dry eyes. Teag helped me conceive a reply most of which he wrote and I duly nodded at.

"Raeyan, it's freezing out here. Why didn't you wait inside?"

"Why didn't you shave your face faster?" Teag woke me from my reflections and I make sure to respond quickly, all smiles and attitude, so he won't notice that I've been day dreaming — behavior he and Dr. Brod treat like a deadly sin since Arly's death.

"I don't want to cut myself," Teag replies. He raises a hand to touch his face before remembering he has his helmet on. He laughs at the fruitless gesture and powers up his board. Seconds later we are rushing over the tundra, chilling wind rushing around our helmets. The heard comes into view and we stop when we get to a safe distance. We pull our boards a little closer now in case we have to get away quickly. I wiggle my latex wrapped toes in the snow and take in the heard. All seems normal except for one thing.

"What is that?" Teag has seen it too.

"I don't know," I say, squinting at the small mountain of what appears to be ice sitting in the middle of the gathered Rhaapiti. "Let's just go about as usual and work our way in."

Teag nods and removes his revolver.

I approach Pegasus with caution. He seems just as relaxed as he always does when I come to him but I don't trust the cool exterior. Hadn't he seen me slay his mate after she trampled Arly? Doesn't he have some secret plot to do me in too? I thought it must be the case. There was no reason for Appletini to attack so the Rhaapiti, which we are still only beginning to understand, must have some violent side usually dormant.

Pegasus let me draw his blood and he shook his massive shoulders and head from side to side when I had finished before returning to digging up frost root. I continue on, keeping pace with Teag who is eager to get to the unknown mass of ice at the center of the heard. His curiosity gets him there before me and he is already kneeling in the snow beside it when I get to him.

"It's the Rhaapiti corpse," he says. The Rhaapiti migrate daily, making their slow, repetitive rotation around the pole of Pioter 7. We track them via tags each morning and send the boards to their location. After Arly died we hadn't gone out for a few days and by the time we did get back in the field the Rhaapiti had moved far away from the corpse. Dr. Brod had wanted to retrieve the corpse but an Alpha Female was a lot of weight to carry and we didn't have the equipment for it so the body had been left to rot. Or so we assumed. Instead of a slowly decomposing Rhaapiti body there was this massive pile of crystals. It seems like the crystals had grown side by side and then one on top of each other, climbing higher and higher until the body was covered entirely by the dazzling white stones.

"What is it?" I ask Teag, reaching out to touch the crystalline mountain that towers a foot above my head. I wipe my thumb across one crystal, wiping away the layer of frost that gives them their opaque appearance, and discover that they are as clear as glass.

Teag is circling the mound and called to me from the opposite side, I can see the hazy outline of his tall body through the crystals. "I'm not sure. It seems to be acting like a fungus, growing on top of the dead flesh but I've never seen anything like it."

"I thought you were supposed to be a biologist?"

He walks back around to meet me. "A zoologist," he says, removing the scythe from his back. "I study animals not plants or mold."

"What are you doing with that?"

Teag begins scrapping the side of one of the crystals. "Taking back a sample."

I watch him continue to scrap the stone. The metal tool is making a hideous screeching noise but he doesn't get any closer to breaking any off. I remove my own scythe and bring the blade down hard against the join where two crystals have merged together. A large crystal, about the length of my arm and the width of my thigh breaks off and falls to the snow. Teag jumps back, startled by my sudden attack but nods thankfully, retrieves the crystal and stuffs it under his arm like he is carrying a tired, chubby dog that just couldn't make the walk around the block.

"Let's get this back to Dr. Brod," he says. "It might give some really ground breaking insights into the nature of the Rhaapiti's blood and biological make up."

"Will it be so ground breaking as to make our jobs obsolete?" I ask.

Teag frowns. "Probably not."

"Well then let's finish up first and you and the good doctor can drool over it like the nerds you are later."

Teag puts the crystal by his board and then gets back to work. It is the fastest I have ever seen him collect since he's started. I guess he just needed the right motivation.

Three days later and three consecutive days of eating breakfast alone I hunt down Teag after scarfing down my smoothie and mango yogurt. I find him in the first place I look, in the lab with Dr. Brod.

"You two have been nearly hinged at the hip since that rock came in here," I say, making my presence known as I lean against the door frame where I can't accidentally tamper with any of Dr. Brod's technical looking equipment, something I have been accused of (and not entirely unjustly) many times before.

Teag looks up from the microscope lens he has been staring into and gives me a big smile I am sure only a toddler in a toy store could muster. He looks over his shoulder at Dr. Brod who hasn't budged from his own microscope since I've come in, then he quietly hurries over to me at the doorway with a clip board in his long green hands.

"I think I've found something," he whispers.

I raise an eyebrow at him. "Is it a secret?"

He shakes his head. "I just want to be sure before I tell Dr. Brod."

"Is this that ground breaking thing you were talking about?"

He nods. "I found an anomaly in the Rhaapiti's blood, a DNA strand that looked very similar to a compound I saw on one of Dr. Brod's charts which details the toxicity of the atmosphere."

"I have no idea what you're talking about, Teag. In laymen's terms please."

"The existing hypothesis about the Rhaapiti is that they are toxic because of the toxic atmosphere and they've just adapted to live in it but when I examined the crystals that grew on the body I found them to also be producing the toxin. So it's the Rhaapiti that produce the toxin and make the atmosphere the way it is."

"So?" I ask. "Why is that important? It seems like the chicken and the egg problem."

"It is but you see the organisms that live

there, though they may be few, depend on the toxicity in the atmosphere to survive. Without it the planet would die because the cloud of toxic fumes in the atmosphere protect it from warming up. If it warmed up then the ice would melt which would shrink the size of the planet nearly in half and it would lose its gravity."

"That isn't going to happen right?" I have a horrible mental image of all the buildings on Pioter 7 slowly lifting off and floating away to hover aimlessly in space.

"Not unless the Rhaapiti stop producing the toxin."

"Good to know." I turn to leave but Teag grabs my arm to stop me.

"Don't you know what this means?" he asks, his eyes wide. "The planet and the Rhaapiti are mutually dependent. Pioter 7 is entirely in balance with its life forms in a way that doesn't exist on any other known planet."

"Cool."

Teag sighs.

I give him an apologetic shrug.

"Raeyan, could you help me with something?"

"Depends what it is."

"I need to analyze the body again, the

actual body, not the crystal structure. So I need a way to get at it."

I think about the tools we have in the weapons room. Most are strictly geared toward working with the Rhaapiti in some manner not for rock fungus removal. But there is one thing I have in mind, a weakness I had heard about from a conversation with Fil who is a pilot of one of the new ships. The so called indestructible material couldn't take the heat.

"I think I have something that might work."

After we finish collecting blood from the herd we set out towards the corpse. We put our boards in the snow and I pick up the flame thrower I carried on the back of mine.

"You're sure this will work?" Teag asks.

"No idea but it's the best I could come up with." I put my thumb over the switch. "Teag, this toxic atmosphere isn't flammable right?"

Teag laughs. "Do you think I'd let you drag a flame thrower all the way out here if it was?"

"Just checking." I flip the switch and aim towed the crystal mound. A heavy stream of flames erupts from the nozzle.

"Remember not to burn the corpse," Teag says, raising his voice above the roar of the fire. Nothing happens for a few minutes and I begin to think I'm wasting my time but then Teag points excitedly to a point on the crystal where it has begun to melt. After that things move much faster and soon all the crystal is a puddle around the corpse. We wait for the crystalline liquid to cool. It takes less than a minute for it to solidify again, two before it is cool enough to touch. The body is in surprisingly good condition and appears almost like it's sleeping if it wasn't for the massive gash in its thick neck.

Teag kneels down beside the body while steam is still rising from the melted crystal and a hissing noise can be heard like when you put a hot pot under the cold tap. He takes a long knife from his belt, not something he typically carries, and inspects the creatures wound.

"What are you going to do?" I ask, putting the flame throwing back on my board to cool.

"I want a sample of its flesh. I need to examine the pores and get a blood sample."

"Like we don't have enough of those?" I shake the pack at my hip, clinking the vials of blood together.

"The blood needs to be from the same organism as the flesh. I just need to find a soft spot."

"The neck is the only spot."

Teag runs his fingers along the Rhaapiti's belly and then jabs his knife into the flesh. It buries in with surprising ease and he continues to rip open the skin until he's made an incision about a foot in length. He sits back on his heels and looks at the damage before sticking the tip of his knife into the incision and prompting it apart. Suddenly a rush of blood and guts spills out of the hole. I step back and Teag scrambles out of the way. There is a large bubble of gross goop in amongst the gore and it slides across the slippery crystal puddle, stopping at Teag's feet.

"What is that disgusting ball?" I ask, pointing at it with my toe.

He kneels down and, to my horror, prods it with his blade. It jiggles but doesn't burst or splatter us with blood as I had imagined it might.

"Not sure," Teag says. "I'm taking it back to the lab."

"Whatever, as long as it's on your board and not mine."

He pulls a large clear bag from his pack and with some difficulty puts the slimy ball into it. The he takes another smaller bag, cuts a hunk of flesh from the Rhaapiti and places it inside.

"Okay mission accomplished." I turn to go back to my board and come face to face with a very live Rhaapiti. I scramble away from it, trying to keep my footing on the crystal and pull my scythe from my back, waving it before me. The beast stares at me unmoving. It doesn't seem hostile but it can't be trusted.

"Whoa." Teag steps between me and the Rhaapiti, hands raised in a gesture of surrender.

"Teag, move!"

"No it's alright, she's not going to hurt us." He holds out his left hand to the Rhaapiti, his palm hovering below its nose. It sniffs him, snorts, and turns to amble off across the tundra.

"What the hell, Teag? You could have gotten us both killed."

"You've been so jumpy around them since Arly died, Raeyan. I think maybe you're just afraid."

I return my scythe. "You didn't even know me before Arly died."

"I know that, I just mean you seemed so confident with them, Dr. Brod says so too, but that's not what I see."

"I'm sorry I'm trying to keep us alive." I stomp off towards by board, brushing shoulders with him as I pass. He collects his bags and follows after me.

"I think they mourn, Raeyan," he tells me when he gets to his board. I already have mine powered up.

"What are you talking about?"

"I think that's why that Rhaapiti was here, so far away from the herd. They never leave the others but that one did and it came directly to the dead Rhaapiti. They might be capable of remorse."

"They're big dumb animals, Teag, they don't know what it's like to lose someone. Not like I do." I take off toward base, leaving Teag behind me. He knows the way.

The weak stream of hot water running down on me feels great after the harsh clinical bath. I rest my forehead against the glass and close my eyes so I can't see the rest of my tiny room which is all too reminiscent of my college dorm for my liking. My bed, shower, and unused desk all occupy the small space leaving me only a little section of floor where I can through down a mat and do some basic exercises; apparently a gym facility wasn't high on the IPM priority list.

I'm tired and my heart was only just starting to regain its normal rhythm. As much as I hate to admit it Teag was right. I had been terrified today and I never used to be. I had enjoyed the company of the Rhaapiti and their typically calm natures. I shouldn't have snapped at Teag and I really needed to get over what happened to Arly and to stop blaming the Rhaapiti. If that was possible.

My doors slid open and Teag came sprawling into my room, stumbling over the threshold.

"Raeyan!"

I practically jump out of the shower in a rush to rip my towel from the hook on the wall.

"Don't you knock on your planet?" I suddenly felt a little less guilty about my treatment of him earlier. It's hard to be sorry while covering your nakedness from an intruder.

"Oh! I'm sorry," He stammers as I witness the phenomenon of blush beneath green skin again.

"Someone better be dying," I say through clenched teeth.

"The planet is dying."

"What?"

"I just finished looking at the samples I brought back and it turns out the Rhaapiti aren't naturally toxic but they get the toxicity from the food they eat, the frost root, and it gets into their blood stream and then is let into the atmosphere through their pores. But we are taking their blood Raeyan, so they have to eat twice as much to replenish the blood supply only there isn't enough frost root for that, it doesn't grow that fast. So we just tested the atmosphere and it's losing toxicity at an alarming rate and the planets temperature is warming up."

"Slow down. Do you mean the whole melting and loss of gravity thing is about to happen?"

"Well it's about two weeks away but yes, that's what I'm implying."

"Turn around."

"What?"

"Turn around I'm getting dressed."

Teag spun around and I remove my towel to use on my hair instead. I quickly wrap it up, turban style, and slip into the jeans and tank top I had left out on the bed and thank god for indoor heating as I leave my socks on the bed and step into my red flip flops.

"Okay let's go talk to Dr. Brod and see what the plan is for this emergency."

"We've come up with a few possible options but none of them are very solid," Teag says, following me from my steamy room.

"My plan involves immediate evacuation. How long would that take?"

Teag frowns. "Three weeks."

"Shit."

Dr. Brod was flipping through pages in a binder laying open on his desk and mumbling like a mad man.

"Doctor please tell me Teag has lost his mind and the doom and gloom story he just gave me is not actually happening."

"Teag may have just saved your life," Dr. Brod replies, not looking up from the binder.

"Yeah, if I'm lucky enough to get on the first ship out of here."

"That is the problem," Dr. Brod says.

"So how do we fix it?"

"Well right now the best I have is killing the Rhaapiti and burning the bodies so that the toxin is released into the atmosphere."

"I have multiple problems with that plan,"

I say. "First off, me and Teag are the only two here qualified to kill a Rhaapiti and I'm the only one with hands on experience, not to mention it would be extremely dangerous because killing one ticks off the whole herd. Secondly, that will only fix the problem temporarily, right? What do we do after we kill all the Rhaapiti? What keeps the atmosphere stable then?"

"Nothing," Dr. Brod says. "But it gives us enough time to get everyone off the planet."

"That's insane."

"It's our only option." Dr. Brod removes his glasses and squeezes the bridge of his nose with his forefinger and thumb. "We can't start tonight, it's already too dark. I'm going to dinner and you will start in the morning."

With that he left me and Teag alone in the lab.

"Is he serious?"

"I don't see any other way," Teag says.

"How did you find out it was the frost root and that the Rhaapiti don't just produce the toxin naturally? Like snakes and jelly fish."

He hesitates. "That ball I collected today was a fetus. That Rhaapiti that killed Arly was pregnant. I tested its blood and it didn't contain the toxin. The mother must have some way of only sharing clean blood with the baby. So I decided to test their food because some animals get characteristics from what they eat, like flamingos, and sure enough that's where the toxin originates."

Pregnant. Appletini had just been protecting her baby. Her condition had made the heard anxious. Our presence that day must have pushed them over the edge. Arly was right, they weren't violent, just protective of their family.

I bite my cheek, thinking. "Can't we just burn a bunch of frost roots and get the toxin out that way?"

Teag shakes his head. "We tried that, there's something about the way it is processed through the Rhaapiti's bodies and pores that create the effect."

"So the whole planet runs off stupid potatoes." I sigh and slump down into Dr. Brod's desk chair. Then I jump up again almost immediately, grabbing Teag by the shoulders.

"Teag, potatoes!" Teag stares at me with confusion. "You said the Rhaapiti would have to eat twice as much to regain the stable atmosphere right?"

"Yeah, that's right, but there aren't enough frost root."

"Exactly, but what if there were?"

"That would be great," he says hesitantly.

"No need for Rhaapiti genocide?"

"I guess not."

"Where is that frost root you tested?"

Teag goes over to a glass box and removes the white potato-like plant covered in blue eyes.

"You can handle it. We've sterilized it so it's only deadly if you ingest it." He hands me the root.

"Excellent. Come with me."

I leave the lab and lead him to the cafeteria. "I'm not really that hungry, Raeyan," Teag says.

"Good we're not eating." I go into the kitchen and find a surprised chef on the other side of the doors. "Where is your food replication machine?"

"Over there," He says, pointing. "But you can't use that."

I ignore him and go to the machine where a young, apron clad girl is placing a handful of strawberries onto a conveyor belt. I watch as it goes into the machine and then a pile of pink mush appears on the other side. She pushes a reverse button on the conveyor belt and removes the original strawberries then scrapes the mush into a bowl.

"Excuse me but I need this." I step in front of her and place the frost root on the belt as she had done and flip the on switch. I hold my breath as I watch it disappear. A moment later I let out a sigh of relief as I see a perfectly whole frost root appear on the other side. I remove both from the machine and hand them to Teag.

He holds the replicated root up for inspection. "You're a genius."

One particularly rainy fall I had decided to repaint my living room and at the demands of the perfectionist within I had to use primer before applying the horrible pale yellow paint I had picked out with the rationale that it would brighten up the space. So I had spent a whole day drinking coffee and literally watching paint dry. Replicating the frost roots one by one through a painfully slow machine was sort of like that — except we didn't have coffee.

Three days later, spent without sleep and taking turns passing frost roots through the machine, Dr. Brod announced that by his calculations we had enough to feed the heard. Loading them into two huge tarps we carry them between our boards and take them out to the herd's location one after the other, dumping the roots in a pile a short distance away from them. It doesn't take the Rhaapiti long to find their free meal and they clean house in under an hour. Me and Teag sit side by side in the snow, literally freezing our butts off as we watch until the very last one was devoured.

"Well, shows over," Teag says, standing and holding a hand down to help me up.

I accept and he heads for his board. I hesitate and then decide I have a goodbye to make; I have no idea if the blood collection project will continue which means my time on Pioter 7 may be at an end. I walk back across the snow to Pegasus who stands watch as always over his heard of full bellied Rhaapiti. I hold my palm up to his nose and he snorts into it, saying hello. I pat the side of his face and then bring my fishbowl to rest against his forehead as I had done with Arly. He snorts again and soon pulls away to nuzzle my pack at my hip before casually walking back to his family. Me and Teag leave them and return to base.

"What now?" I ask as Teag and Dr. Brod stand looking at graphs on multiple computer screens in the lab.

"Pray, if you must," Dr. Brod says, removing his glasses.

"We just have to wait and see if the levels of toxicity in the atmosphere return to normal," Teag elaborates, pointing out a red and white graph consisting of only one bar. "When this hits five hundred, we're safe."

"And if it doesn't?"

People always say weightlessness is a good feeling like when a problem has been taken off your shoulders. "The weight has been lifted", they'll say, "it feels great". Everyone wants to lose weight, shed pounds, remove layers – "I feel ten pounds lighter". No one mentions the chest crushing, heart thumping panic of true weightlessness. The out of body feeling that signifies total loss of control.

A sound reaches my ears through the darkness and a sudden blinding light throws gravity back under my feet, like it was rug, removed only temporarily so it could be beat free of dust and then laid down again beneath my feet.

"Rise and shine, Raeyan."

I groan and toss a pillow at my intruder before burying my head under the blankets. The sheets are jerked away from me again and I blink up at the green face grinning down at me.

"Still a little jet legged?" Teag asks.

The days are longer and the sun rises earlier on Pioter 7 and my sleep cycle still hasn't adjusted yet. I arrived back at the now nearly empty Sapron Hollow base two days ago – four Acroniatera days. Teag and his group of fellow scientists gave me a warm welcome before I crashed and slept for an uninterrupted eight hours, but adjustment time is over and Teag is making sure I'm not slacking.

He leaves me and I crawl out of my warm bed, dress, devour two nutrient bars (no more potatoes for me), and join the others outside after suiting up. The revolvers still hang on the white wall of the armory but I don't take one. I only carry the scythe now and so does Teag. We have to protect the others, all six of them, but now that we better understand the Rhaapiti it's not nearly so dangerous.

Teag's been here for two months already and his team of researchers have learned a lot about the Rhaapiti's mating habits, community dynamics, and a whole bunch of other things I don't entirely understand but Teag insists are important breakthroughs.

There are no solar boards now, no staff to feed us or receive supply shipments which are now infrequent. The suits remain, as well as the revolvers and the scythes: everything they have no need for back home has been abandoned here to our benefit. The IPM hasn't officially stated if the program is closed for good but with the near catastrophe and the so far incurable flaw in the material it doesn't look like Sapron

Hollow will be back up and running anytime soon. Which has opened up a great opportunity for Teag and his bright-eyed colleagues.

I had only been back on Acroniatera for a month when Teag got a hold of me and asked if I'd be willing to tag along with his team. I knew the terrain and I could help protect them. I'd been hesitant to return but I was in need of a job, so I accepted.

The trek across the tundra is long and cold, some others wear parkas over their suits. I have to hug my arms to keep from shivering. In a week I'll become acclimated but right now a week feels like a very long time.

Teag jogs up behind me and throws an arm around my shoulders.

"Glad to be back yet?" Teag asks, winking at me.

The heard is in view now, Pegasus's silhouette the largest against the rising sun. I cannot yet see his new mate that Teag told me of but I know she must be close. I wonder if Pegasus will walk out and meet me as he sometimes used to do.

I smile, squinting against the brilliance of the tundra. "Actually, I am."

THE COLOUR OF GOLD

Noon's sun danced across the sand in waves, making the still distant walls of Missky appear to sway like a Nazark dancer, hips shifting in one direction, chest in the other, skirts lifting off the ground to reveal the strips of leather tied around each ankle, laden with large bells of bronze.

The thought of bells reminded Nado he was hungry. He turned on his thin brown horse and used his riding crop to smack the string of chimes attached to one of the saddle bags. They chimed constantly as he rode, imitating the soft trickle of a stream, but when struck they reached a pitch almost beyond hearing. The horse snorted and shook his head, sending his blonde main flopping from side to side.

Deer was a skittish mount, aptly named. Nado calmed him, patting the side of the animal's neck where a discolouration of his coat made it appear he carried an image of the sun.

Nado chose horses the same way he chose wine—if they were easy on the nose, they were fine by him. He knew fiercely little about horses or wine. He wouldn't have bought a new mount at all, but then it would have taken him three days to get from his home to the Capital, rather than one, and King Casimir would have him leeched to death if he didn't make it to Missky within a day of being summoned.

With Deer calm again Nado retrieved a strip of smoked salmon from a saddle bag. He ripped a piece off with his teeth, keeping the other, larger half in one hand.

A screech from the sky had Nado looking down. It was too bright to look up with the sun at its peak, but it was just as easy to spot Saljack's shadow as it was to spot the bird himself.

The hawk possessed an impressive six foot wingspan but cast a far greater shadow. Nado watched the gray shape coast across the white sand, wings still save for the occasional powerful flap. The sight always made Nado think of dragons long dead, and even when they had lived the ones around Missky would have been wyrms, wingless monsters that flew only on the sands. Still captivating to the imagination of a boy who'd been born long after the era of the Great Beasts, but not nearly as impressive as wings.

As the shadow gradually shrunk, turning from dragon into eagle into hawk, Nado looked up, despite the glare, and tossed the other half of salmon into the air.

The sun only burned his eyes a moment

before Saljack blocked it out, snatching the smoked meat from the sky. His silver body was aglow with the backlight of the sun, as if his body really did possess the fire of his ancient ancestors.

Eight black scimitar talons wrapped around the staff tied horizontally onto the horse's rump, just behind the saddle. The horse snorted again, stamping his front feet to show his excitement. Saljack cried in response, his bottomless eyes glistening as they peered at Nado.

"Shhhh," Nado said, giving the sunspot on the horse's neck another gentle pat.

There was a tug at the sleeve of Nado's robe. He jerked his arm back just before Saljack could nip him with his beak.

"Enough, Saljack, Deer is new. He is not used to being ridden by beasts," Nado explained.

Saljack cried again, rousing his feathers.

"Beasts with talons, then." Nado stroked Saljack's head with the top of his knuckles, feeling the bird push against him, much like a cat would. The Missky hawks had a peculiar way of going gray like humans did. Every feather on his body was as silver as the moon. Nado had once thought it was a natural phenomenon, like the bird's strange brackish scent expunged from his feathers everytime he took flight, but he later came to learn the real cause. Magic.

Nado wasn't a religious man. He held no favour with any creed or cult. It wasn't that he disliked magic on principle, it simply seemed wrong to him. Unnatural. The revelation that there was some magical connection to the Missky hawks had almost made him part ways with Saljack, but he'd become too fond of the bird by then. Nado told himself it was the boyish fantasies of dragons...but perhaps the bird reminded him of other things too.

With no warning, Saljack screeched and spread his wings. In one whoosh he was in the air again, sending Nado floundering for the reins to keep Deer in line. He'd just regained control of the startled horse when he noticed his view of the dancing walls of Missky, the City of Sand and Shade, had changed. A small black shimmering shape stood between him and the gates, a shape that was growing, coming closer.

A rider.

A sickening feeling took root in Nado's chest. The city never sent a rider to meet him. He was no merchant, no lord, no brigand. Perhaps it was the new mount, perhaps even with their spyglasses they couldn't be certain.

No. He was only one man. They would wait until he reached the gate to identify him.

They would never send a rider.

The dust the rider kicked up marred all views of the gates he'd left. As he got closer Nado could see he was young, a wall cadet, rarely given any task beyond fetching water and certainly nothing outside the gates of the city, not even so small a thing as meeting a doctor.

The cadet's gray steed came to a stomping halt, overshooting Nado by so much that he was forced to loop around him, pulling up beside Nado as they both faced the city.

Both horses pranced and snorted as Nado and the cadet held tight to their reins.

"Are you doctor Nado Gaj?" the cadet asked. He had a high, shaking voice and bright eyes filled with the intensity of youth. Nado wasn't so old, but he knew he'd lost that light years ago.

"I am. I've come to tend to the prince," Nado said.

"He's dead."

Nado stared back at the cadet, waiting for words to follow, words that would make those first two make sense. But he remained silent.

"Dead?" Nado asked, shaking his head. "I don't understand. I got word yesterday he'd developed a mild cough. The start of something, likely just a seasonal sickness. There was no urgency in the letter. No other symptoms. Nothing that would suggest—"

"He's dead, sir," the cadet said. There was a helpless sadness to his speech. He'd likely never laid eyes on the prince but from afar, looking up at a platform or balcony, or perhaps as he passed in parade.

"The King hopes you will see him all the same."

"Of course, of course. Take me to him immediately."

The cadet nodded and spurred his horse back toward the gates. Nado did likewise. The beating hooves left a cloud in their wake, sending the gently waving sands into a storm.

Missky was a solitary city built on the coast of a sequestered stretch of desert periodically called home by pirates. The Godskyi family had turned the barren land into a paradise. The Godskyis boasted that they'd once been royalty of the far off Catbik Empire, but it was far more likely they were pirates who'd tired of the sea, staking claim to a bit of land no one else saw any value in.

Inside the gates Nado typically relinquished his mount to a guard. They knew him and the stables took good care of his horses. But today, the cadet passed right by the guard's station and charged into the midday market crowds. He yelled ahead, clearing a path for them, and Nado was surprised at the speed and graciousness with which the masses parted. Cadet or not, the people here had an innate respect, bordering on primal devotion, for the green and gold of the Godskyi royalty.

Nado kept his eyes on that green and gold vest the cadet wore so as not to lose him and be swallowed up by the crowds. The symbolism behind the royal colours was simple: gold for the relentless sun, and green for the miraculous abundance of plant life within the walls.

Ferns grew in pots the size of tubs, and trees stretched toward the very sun that should have dried them to ash. Dangling drapes of leaves cascaded off stone balconies or over the edge of rooftops, creating shaded alcoves. Bushes grew flowers that blossomed in a city that knew only one season.

The notorious maxim of the Godskyis was Life and Lucre. Nado looked up at the arch as they entered the exterior palace grounds where that very motto was etched in stone. Life and lucre, gold and green—but which colour represented which affirmation? In almost every other royal crest gold would equate wealth, but anyone who found the fortune to walk the streets of Missky would surely see that her wealth was her life. The city breathed.

But somewhere its prince does not.

The walls of the palace rose up before them and the impressive golden gate strewn with climbing black ivy. The entire length of the walls were bathed in the black which was both poisonous and possessed razor thorns. It was an intimidating defense, yet its beauty had a way of masking its deadly purpose.

The streets were as they usually were, bustling. People bartered, others begged. Children ran and laughed or clung to their mothers' skirts. But there was no fear or sadness, no unusual excitement. No one stopped to stare at the walls and ponder, or to cast a sigh or a prayer in their direction. They didn't yet know their prince was dead. This was not a city in mourning, but one merely about its business.

The gates began to draw open as they approached. The cadet did not wait for their old joints to creak wide open, but instead urged his mount through a gap only just wide enough for the horse's shoulders. Nado, following close behind, pressured his far more timid mount to do the same, only at the last moment remembering his staff and reaching back to slide it swiftly from it's fastenings, holding it beside him just as they squeezed through so close to the gold bars that Nado could smell the sour scent of the ivy.

Within the walls hung quite a different atmosphere. Guards stood sentinel at the palace steps, their backs straighter than if they'd been tied to boards. And there were so many of them. Nado looked around the courtyard as he brought his horse to a stop. There were guards along the walls, both above and on the ground. They stood in the shade of the entrance balconies, shadows moving between the stone pillars. Missky practiced what they called Vunderkol. Because the city got so hot, they had to take frequent breaks from their labours where they would rest in the shade, napping or drinking Kol, the sweet wine that was one of the city's main exports. These breaks occurred several times a day and each had its own name. There was Ry, Ry-kol, Men, Leev, and Shad. Typically only a handful of guards would be on duty at Men, the longest break of the day, but now the courtyard was filled with them. And all their eyes were on Nado.

One of the guards approached to take Nado's mount. He handed down the reins. The cadet slid off the back of his horse, boots striking the thick packed sand of the courtyard. "He's in the King's chambers, Doctor Gaj," the cadet said. "King Casimir said you're to go right up."

Nado hiked up his robes and slid off Deer's back, staff still in one hand. He wore a satchel across his chest which carried most of his medicines, though he'd no longer be needing them today.

The cadet gave Nado a curt bow in way of parting and turned on his heel in a swift fashion that was custom of the Godskyi guards, a discipline drilled into them at a young age. Before he could take his next step however, Nado had him by the collar of his vest.

"Saddle bag," Nado said, pushing the youth in the direction of Deer, who was already being escorted out of the courtyard toward the stables. "The left one. Bring it."

The cadet went hurrying off after the horse as Nado climbed the steps. Robes in one hand, staff in the other. The guards nodded at him as he passed, chins to chest, a sign of respect that was reserved for the elderly, or for wisemen and doctors. It made Nado feel old. He was likely only a year or two older than most of these guards yet they treated him as if he were ancient. He used to ignore the gesture, but he'd learned to accept it. He was young for a doctor of his caliber, but his intelligence didn't make him fragile, even if his staff and long robes often made him appear debilitated.

The palace was quiet. Servants gathered in corners watching Nado as he passed, their whispers gathering like cobwebs. Nado swept past them.

The King's chambers were on the top floor, up a wide spiraling staircase covered with a soft green carpet. Nado paused before the doors when he reached the top. They were rich oak, dark, carved with images of ships on a sprawling sea. This was not the first tragedy

Nado had attended behind those doors.

He didn't knock. He pushed the doors wide and went in.

The chambers were fuller than he'd anticipated. King Casimir was on the balcony smoking. The strong smell of tobacco mingled with the musky incense that burned on either side of the massive bed. Lumir, The King's bastard, sat in a chair against the wall beside the doors. Four guards stood around him. His dark hair was pulled back into a braid starting from his forehead and ending at the nap of his neck. His eyes were puffy and bloodshot from crying. He sat silently, but his chest heaved and spasmed as he attempted to kept more tears at bay.

Five serving girls stood along the right wall wearing green body suits beneath sheer gold dresses. The eldest, who stood closest to the head of the bed, was the only one who didn't have a tear streaked face, but her hands shook around the silver water pitcher she held.

Nado looked to the balcony. Casimir turned, met his eyes, and turned back, resting his elbows on the balcony rail and looking out over his city. Nado sighed and leaned his staff against the wall as a tall thin man came to shut the door behind him. The man's name was Jug and he was an advisor to Casimir, one Nado wasn't fond of. And the feeling was mutual. But for once Jug said nothing as Nado got settled.

Nado set his satchel on the long cushioned stool at the foot of the bed and shrugged out of his outer robe, leaving only a tan tunic. Each of his arms were murals of inked anchors, ships, swords, coins, and women. The black images traveled onto the rest of his body as well, though rarely saw the light of day when he was anywhere outside his home.

Casimir employed only the best doctors, musicians, soldiers, and architects, even if they were ex-pirates, though he highly discouraged those in his employ from making such facts public.

Nado allowed his gaze to rest on the scene he had more or less evaded. The King's massive bed was laden with an opulence of blankets, silks, and pillows in shades of deep greens embroidered with gold and silver threads and beading. And at its center lay the small, still body of the eight year old Prince Momir.

Nado walked to the side of the bed opposite the serving girls and took Momir's thin wrist in his hand, searching for a pulse. His skin was cold to the touch. His heart had surely stopped beating many hours ago.

The boy's russet skin was devoid of its usual warm glow. His dark locks were slicked to his head and the blankets beneath him showed signs he'd been bathed in sweat. His eyes were closed, dots of gold powder on the lids showed one of the serving girls had shut them, likely wiping at her own powdered eyes before closing the boy's.

Nado turned to Lumir, still sitting silently in the corner, surrounded by guards with hands on their weapons.

"Casimir," he said, crossing his arms. "Is this necessary?"

The King didn't turn from the balcony. When he didn't reply, Jug took his silence as permission to speak for him.

"He's the only person with motive to kill the boy," Jug said in his peculiarly deep voice. It was the satin drawl of Nazark, as was his dark skin and slim features.

Nado glared at the royal advisor. "Him, all the nobility of Yeg, Kafgrad, and Morz who would love to see Missky destabilized, extremists of the Oracle of Broph or the Khor Order both of whom deny his God, and every blasted pirate who docks on these shores with some lunacy aspiration to put a crown on his own head."

Jug clasped his hands behind his back. "Lumir is the eldest, first born, and if he weren't born out of wedlock he'd be heir of Missky. With his brother out of the way and the Queen long dead Casimir would have little choice but to name him his successor."

"I didn't kill him!" Lumir gasped, voice

hoarse from sobbing. "He's my baby brother. I don't want to be king. I love him!"

Casimir set his cigar in a gold plated tray on the balcony and turned to face the room. He wasn't a large figure, but he had the constitution of a man used to demanding the attention of an audience. He'd always reminded Nado of an actor, or rather the kind of man actors often pretended to be. Despite that, he was not a man for theater, or spectacle for spectacle's sake. When the people of Missky were finally told of their prince's death it would be a brief, quiet affair. A short procession and a quick burial. The people would be free to leave flowers at the mausoleum but Casimir wouldn't allow them to pile up for long. No matter the magnitude of his heart break for Momir, it would not alleviate his sense of decorum.

Nado looked at Lumir and shook his head. He was the reason Nado had any relationship to the royal family. Lumir had been just a boy when Nado had docked at Missky. You couldn't just leave a pirate ship. You couldn't just decide to get off at the next port and start a new life. That's what they sold you when you joined on, but in reality the captain owned you, the sea owned you. The only way to leave a ship was the plank or in a casket. Or if no one else lived to tell of your departure.

Nado had been aboard the Black Tide for eight years alongside his sister Onra. They're mother had been a doctor and when she'd died they both took her skills to sea, thinking they could both help and make a fortune doing it. They'd been wrong. They were more deckhands than doctors most of the time, nursing the odd infection or cold. It was only when Onra began to be used for other things that Nado decided they had to abandon ship. He'd poisoned their ale the night before they docked. The crew all left the ship to seek pleasures and entertainment on land, and all dropped dead within hours, scattered about the streets, bars, and brothels of Missky. It had been a scandal for the city, shrouded in mystery. Establishments that had one of the cursed pirates take his last breath under their roof boasted of it by hanging a plaque above the door, painted with the masthead of the Black Tide; a mermaid with a turquoise tiara and ebony skin.

After slinking off the ship Nado and Onra had made an effort to ask about those plaques, as if never having heard of the ship. They never admitted to being on it. Even those who saw the ink on their arms that clearly marked them for pirates never associated them with the Black Tide, not even the King.

Casimir had found Nado in the back room of an alehouse where Nado had been working as a doctor for months while his sister collected herbs for him, her hands becoming blistered and cut, her skin red and raw from long days under the hot sun, picking from the thorny bushes that lined the coast of Missky. All the while allowing Nado's hands to remain steady and pristine.

Casimir had not looked like a king then, only like a desperate father. Lumir, a boy of eight, was sick with fever, red bumps all over his skin from a rash no one else had been able to identify.

For Nado it had been an easy diagnosis. The boy was allergic to a type of imported garlic, a garlic he had seen often while traveling on the Black Tide. Many people had a reaction to it and it could be deadly, but was simple to treat. He provided a salve for the rash and an elixir to counteract the garlic. The boy recovered quickly.

Casimir had returned to the alehouse as King, wearing his royal livery, and requested Nado and his sister come to stay in the palace to work for him. Onra had happily obliged, but Nado saw it as being captive again and he didn't like his odds of being able to kill off the entire royal family.

He agreed to work for Casimir, but not exclusively. Casimir reluctantly agreed, and gave him land on the outskirts of Missky, far from the city, where Nado could care for other towns and fishing villages.

He'd often been called back to the city. At first he'd always made an effort to see Onra, but as she grew older and joined the Missky Priestesses, an order Nado wasn't fond of, they'd grown apart. Casimir and his children had become more family to him than his own blood. He'd watched the boys grow up, mending everything from broken bones to skinned knees. Nado knew Lumir would never hurt his brother.

Casimir walked to the bed, brushing a hand against Momir's brow. "The Priestesses said it was too late to bring him back, even with their medicine."

Nado just managed to hold back a scoff. Medicine. More like magic. Their arts were unnatural. Nado knew the workings of the human body inside and out, so well that in some places they said what he did was magic too. But it wasn't. It was knowledge. Years of study and practice. Magic was too akin to prayer for his liking, wishing on a coin tossed in a well. Something about it made his skin crawl, particularly when it had to do with bringing people back from death.

Without turning from Momir, Casimir waved his hand dismissively at the guards around Lumir. "At ease."

"Your Highness—" Jug protested, but Casimir silenced him with a glare.

"I lost one son today, I will not lose another."

A heavy silence fell over the room. Nado stepped forward, considering his next words carefully, knowing they would likely not be appreciated by the present company.

"If I may, I would still like to examine him," Nado said. "I may be able to determine the cause of death."

The silence dragged on until the eldest serving girl quietly spoke up. "There are no wounds," she whispered, staring into her water pitcher.

Nado nodded. So that likely excluded pirates or any outside Kingdom. One of the cults then, or at the very least someone who respected the Missky customs. It was considered a blessing to go to the afterlife as whole as possible. Natural deaths such as illness were considered mercies where a man stabbed to death in the street was greatly pitied. Not only because one took place in bed, surrounded by family and the other was horrific, but because the later meant open wounds. Any visibly torn flesh would have to be stitched up before being granted entry into the afterlife. Those with wounds would have to go to the Jokano, a monster of death who used her needle like fingernails to stitch you up. It was said to be painful, a process that could take years and years, longer even than the time you'd spent among the living. Nado didn't believe it, but everyone else in this room did, and even an assassin wouldn't sentence the boy to that fate if he too were a believer.

"Poison then," Nado said.

Casimir shook his head. "Nadia tastes all his meals, everything on his plate, in his cup, before he brings a morsel to his mouth. But she's fine. She showed no signs of poisoning."

Nado considered that, then his heart lurched. "How old is Nadia?"

Casimir finally turned to look at him. "Thirty...something"

"Forty-two," One of the serving girls corrected.

"Bring her to me," Nado said.

"What?" Jug's brow scrunched in concern. "Why?"

Nado turned to him. "Some poison works faster in children. Much faster."

Casimir motioned to the youngest of the serving girls and she sprinted from the room, not even bothering to bow, golden dress trailing behind her as she pushed through the heavy doors.

"Check the kitchens," Casimir said, addressing one of the guards by Lumir. "See that everyone is accounted for, that no one is harmed or has tried to leave Missky. Speak to the newest hires, where they came from and when."

The guard nodded, gave a curt bow and departed.

Nado looked at Momir again, skin pale, eyes closed as if in sleep. He watched his chest, willing it to move, wishing for him to once again draw breath.

The doors rushed open again as the serving girl returned with Nadia. She was a tall woman, who looked much younger than her forty-two years if that number was indeed correct. Nado went to her immediately, taking her chin in his hands. She didn't struggle, didn't so much as flinch. Nado pushed a strand of pale blonde hair from her face, planting the back of his hand against her forehead, feeling for heat. He looked in her eyes, pale blue, cloudy, red at the corners. He put his nose close to her face.

"Breath," he said. She obliged, opening her mouth and blowing out a soft breath.

He stepped back and nodded. "Thank you, Nadia."

She waited a moment, hesitating, waiting for him to say more. When he didn't, she looked to Casimir. When he too remained silent, she made a shaky bow, turned on her heel, and left. The serving girl escorted her out, shutting the doors behind them.

"It could have been her, if not the kitchens," Jug said.

"No," Nado said. "It wasn't her. Not unless she was determined enough to follow him into death."

Jug's eyes widened. "She's poisoned? But she looks fine."

Nado shivered slightly, still smelling the acrid odor of her breath, the damp touch of her skin. "She isn't fine. Her symptoms will only worsen."

"Is there anything that can be done?" Casimir asked.

"If I knew the poison I may be able to provide an antidote."

"How can you determine the poison?"

Nado shook his head. "If the food remained—"

"It doesn't." Jug said.

"Who ate with him when he had the last meal before he showed signs of sickness?" Nado asked.

"I did," Lumir said, sniffling. "We had smoked duck and cheese and nuts."

Riding food, Nado noted. "You were hunting?"

Lumir nodded. "Servants accompanied us, we all ate when we made camp."

"Did you pack your own saddle bags?" Casimir asked.

Lumir thought about it. "Yes. Well, except for the tea."

"Tea?" Nado asked. "Was Nadia among the servants?"

"Of course."

"And she ate the food as well?"

"Yes, before we even sat down for lunch."

"Did any of the other servants have tea? And did Nadia taste it?"

Lumir closed his eyes in thought. "No other servants had tea, they were packing up while it brewed so we'd be ready to move on. I remember Nadia sitting with a cup though, drinking it before pouring Momir's. So yes, she must have tasted it."

"What kind of tea was it?"

Lumir shook his head. "I don't know. It was bitter. Earthy. I didn't like it much."

Nado's heart froze in his chest. He glanced at Casimir. The King's eyes had fixed on Lumir, his hand, which had been caressing his deceased son's temple, stopped to hang at his side.

"Lumir," Nado said. "You had the tea too?"

Lumir stared back at him, realization crossing his features.

Nado crossed the room and leaned close to him. "Breath."

Lumir swallowed perceptibly before obeying. His breath was warm and sour. Nado stepped back. He tried to don a clinical expression but his pity must have been apparent because Lumir shuddered and a crash sounded behind them, causing Nado, and everyone else in the room, to jump as Casimir sent a luckily unlit lantern flying off the bedside table and thundering onto the floor.

Momir of course didn't move at the sound, but laid unnaturally still. The stillness of death, Nado reminded himself. He would have to come to terms with the fact that he was a boy no longer, but merely a corpse.

Even Jug was cautious when he spoke next. "Is there any way to discover the poison without the tea?"

Nado stiffened. There was. Before, he may not have mentioned it, but now, with two other lives hanging in the balance, he had no choice.

"I could check his stomach contents." No one said a word, though the faces of the serving girls paled visibly.

"The process is quick. An incision down the abdomen, tie off the tubes to the stomach, sever them—"

One of the serving girl's shoulders pitched forward as she barely held back bile. Cupping a hand to her mouth she looked to the King who nodded, and she left the room.

"The rest of you are dismissed as well," Casimir said, waving at both the girls and the guards. The girls bowed, the guards saluted, and they all left in a stream of green and gold and clinking armor and bracelets. When the doors shut again it was only Nado, Jug, Lumir, and the King who remained with Momir's body.

"You can't honestly intend to cut open the Prince?" Jug said. "To mutilate his body and send him to Jokano?"

"In order to find an antidote I need to find out what poisoned him."

"Do it on me," Lumir said, rushing to his feet, eyes watery and clouded with a mix of fear and determination. "You can look at my stomach contents. Kill me and save Nadia—and avenge my Brother."

Casimir's voice was soft but halting. "If I were to avow human sacrifice it would be Nadia under his knife, not you."

Lumir's eyes widened and he slowly sunk back into his seat.

"I'm not killing anyone," Nado said. "That's preposterous. After death examinations are routine in..." He trailed off.

"In heathen kingdoms?" Jug finished.

Nado skewered him with a glare. In Nazark there was a fairly prominent and completely legal sect who cannibalized their dead. Nado didn't believe Jug to be of their ilk, but he'd certainly lived in that heathen kingdom much of his life. Missky had built its own unique infrastructure, economy, and culture as well as its faith. The religion was not widespread, with few believers outside its walls. Jug had surely adopted the faith as his own when he'd come to Missky. That didn't make him a hypocrite or a fraud, even if Nado thought him both, but it should have given him a little more perspective.

"Is there any way at all to manage what you say without leaving wounds in my son's flesh?" Casimir asked.

Nado was about to answer when the door closed. Nado hadn't even heard it open. The salty tang in the air told him who it was even before she spoke.

"I may be able to help with that, your Highness," Onra said.

Nado turned to watch his sister give Casimir a deep bow in her long blue robes. White waves of hair spilling over her shoulders.

Nado didn't know what sort of magic it was that turned the Priestesses hair white, but he didn't like it. Onra was far too young to have lost her dark locks.

"I want my son to go unmarred into the afterlife," Casimir said.

"And I need to remove his stomach," Nado growled at Onra, challenging her.

Her pretty brown eyes sparkled and the salty scent reached the back of Nado's throat. "It can be done. With magic."

Naked and laid out on a thin stone slab, Momir looked even smaller than he had on his father's massive bed, if that were possible. Lumir had been the one to scoop up his small frame from the bed and carry him to the Deck. That's what they called the hall where they prepared their dead for burial. Nado didn't know why they called it that, but supposed it came from their maritime ancestry. He remembered another deck, bodies crumpling to damp planks as he and Onra watched on.

As if at the thought of her name, Onra came into the Deck then. Everyone else had left them. Even Lumir. Despite Nado's promise not to pierce Momir's flesh, none had been able to bear the idea of his insides being taken out.

"Do you have everything you'll need?" Onra asked, stepping up to the other side of the raised slab.

Nado considered the boy. "I'll need a block, something to put beneath his back to keep the chest up."

She nodded and slipped out of her heavy outer robe. All that was left beneath was a thin white cotton dress, haltered around the neck. It left her arms bare. Like his own, they were painted with images of the life they'd left behind; mermaids, fish, breaching waves, a skull.

Onra folded the fabric of her robe into a tidy pile, using the sleeves to hold it together. She held it up for Nado's approval. He nodded.

Nado slipped a hand under each side of the boy's ribs and lifted him up just enough for Onra to position the robe between his shoulder blades. When Nado set him down again his chest was splayed, arms resting farther from his body, palms almost tilted up. His head rested back, revealing his throat. Nado traced a line with his eyes from one of Momir's shoulders, just beneath the armpit, down toward the breast bone. Then another identical line to mirror that one, making a v-shape. From there he would have cut a line down to the groin, through the top layers of flesh and muscle until he could peel back three separate segments, two flapping over the ribs and the upper segment coming back over the face. Then to cut through bone, removing the rib cage, to reveal the internal organs.

Nado could have done it in his sleep. But he wouldn't have to. No cutting through flesh or bone this time. None the less he laid out his tools on a table he'd pulled up beside him. A scalpel, two lengths of cord, and two bowls; one empty and one filled with water.

"Are you ready?" Nado asked Onra.

She nodded and put her hands gently on Momir's abdomen. "Where can I rest them so I won't be in your way?"

Nado took her hands in his, moving one higher and one lower, giving him enough room to work. Once satisfied he nodded.

Onra closed her eyes and began to chant.

Nado recognized the language as what the Missky people simply referred to as the Old Sounds. If it had ever had a proper name, it had lost it long ago. Nado couldn't make out any of the words but the tune rolled over his skin with trembling familiarity. A shanty. A song of mourning. Of dark and stormy nights, and sunrises spent counting those swept overboard.

The song—the spell—sounded like drowning felt.

Nado watched as Momir's already pale skin grew paler beneath Onra's hands until it was opaque, then entirely pellucid. Nado could see into him; lungs, stomach, intestines, heart, their deep colours now blanched and dull.

He looked up at Onra but her eyes remained shut as she sang.

Nado reached toward Momir's abdomen, fingers gingerly touching the skin. He expected the cool clamminess of death but instead felt only a faint tingling as his fingers went right through. He had his hand inside, beyond the barrier of flesh. He reached a little further but his fingers bounced off the boy's sternum.

Fearing a sudden interruption might break Onra's spell and leave his hand trapped in Momir's chest cavity, Nado pulled back his fingers before speaking. "The bones too," he said.

Onra's song never faltered and Nado watched Momir's ribs turn as translucent as his skin.

Steeling himself, he reached in again, prepared for the tingling sensation of magic, the scent of salt and brine burned his nose, making him want to gag, but he held it back. After years at sea, he'd learned to put it out of mind.

When his fingers grazed the stomach and he felt the flesh of it in his hands his breath caught. He was really performing an examination void of the messy work, the cutting, the sawing, the blood. He could normally avoid much of the blood as it pooled at the bottom of the body without a heart beating to help it defy gravity, but never this clean, never this simple. He was holding Momir's stomach and yet the boy remained intact, remained as if in peaceful sleep on the cold stone, naked like the faery children of Catbik, or like mermaids.

Nado took a piece of his cord and tied off the stomach where it attached to the esophagus. The other cord he tied at the bottom of the stomach just above the small intestine. Then he reached for his scalpel.

Onra did not cease her singing but when Nado turned back her eyes were open, watching. He carefully brought the scalpel through the ethereal skin, muscle, and bone of the abdomen until he reached the stomach. Were he doing a full examination he would have only made a few simple cuts that connected the organs to the muscle tissue, allowing him to remove all the organs as a unit, still connected as they were internally. But for this he needed only the stomach. Two cuts on the outside of each cord had the stomach free. He lifted it up out of the body, carrying it to the table in his left palm, the scalpel still clutched in his right.

Nado held the stomach above the empty

bowl and made a long incision. Bile trickled out. A greenish-yellow semi liquid filled the bottom of the bowl. Before putting the scalpel aside, he used the edge of the blade to pry wide the incision he'd made, looking inside to examine the stomach lining. Onra watched diligently, unphased. They'd seen worse.

He didn't know how long Onra could keep up her spell, didn't know if it tired her, or took anything at all from her, so he did his best to be swift. It was only exterior wounds the Missky determined in need of Jokano's handiwork. But nonetheless Nado decided to return the stomach to its place. He set it back inside the torso, nestled partly beneath the ribs, alongside the liver and kidneys.

He removed the cords at either end and pulled them free of the body.

"You can stop now," Nado said. "It's done."

Almost instantaneously the song stopped, the smell of salt lessened, and Onra pulled her hands from Momir. His skin returned, organs, muscle, and bone no longer visible.

Onra stepped back from the slab, looked up at Nado, then fainted.

Nado rushed around the slab, just barely quick enough to catch her head in his hands, protecting it from cracking against the stone tiles. She was already fluttering her eyes open again as he pulled her head into his lap.

"Onra, are you alright?" Nado asked, brushing aside her white hair from her face. She'd braided it for the procedure, just as she'd done when they were young, but wisps had escaped around her temples.

"Fine," she said. Nado helped her sit up, cradling her against his chest. She tilted her head back to look up at him, and smiled. "Nothing a cup of tea won't fix."

Despite himself, Nado smiled. He didn't know if it was the grisly work of medicine or the pirate's life that had given Onra her macabre sense of humor, but it always had a way of lifting his spirits in the darkest of hours. Like that of a little boy he'd loved laying dead a few feet away.

He sobered and helped Onra to her feet.

"Go," she said, brushing his hands away from her as she regained balance. "My work's done. Yours isn't."

Nado nodded and returned to his table to examine the stomach contents. Using his scalpel once more he probed the substance in the bowl. He found something solid, only partially digested, not yet fully deteriorated by stomach acid. A leaf.

Carefully, he lifted it from the bile and set it on the table, unfolding it to examine its shape.

"Onra," Nado said. "Do you recognize this?"

Onra was in the process of lifting Momir's body in order to shimmy her robe out from under him. Succeeding, she hung the robe over her forearm and joined her brother at the table.

"Hmm," she mused, taking the scalpel from his hand and tracing what was left of the plant's veins.

It looked familiar to Nado but he couldn't place it. It was leathery, harder than anything typically used for tea, even among poisons. He'd be worried he'd find nothing at all in the stomach, that he'd be too late and all traces of the poison would have passed through his system.

"Cove grass," Onra said, setting down the scalpel. "I'm sure of it. It's a seaweed—"

"That grows on the wharf down by the docks," Nado finished. Onra nodded.

"I need to collect some. The antidote is made from the same sap it carries." Nado slipped back into his robes, recovering his tattooed arms. Before he could slip out of the Deck Onra stopped him, handing him her robe.

"I'll come," she said.

He shook out her robe and held it up so she could slip her arms in. "You don't have to,"

Nado said.

"Who else is going to wade into the sea or hang off the wharf?" She asked, cocking a brow as she finished fastening her robe.

"I'm capable," Nado said.

She put a cool, slightly shaky hand to his cheek. "I know."

A salty breeze blew in off the azure sea, mingling with any lasting scent of Onra's magic.

Nado stood on the wharf, hands clasped before him, agitated as he watched his sister, true to her word, wade into the surf up to her thighs. Waves splashed her robes, dampening her hair and skin. People stared. Fishermen forgot about their lines and nets, pirates and sailors watched from prows, sails billowing in the evening wind above them.

"What's a Missky Priestess doing digging for clams?" A nearby man wondered aloud.

Nado didn't correct him. Deer stood nearby, as skittish of the sea as he was of Saljack. "Onra, do you have enough?" Nado asked.

Onra looked up and tossed a handful of cove grass onto the dock. Nado collected the slimy seaweed and tucked it away in one of the many pockets of his robe.

"That will have to do," Onra said. "I'm freezing."

Nado reached down, stretching to get a hold of her. They clasped forearms and he hoisted her up. Water rained from the hem of her robes, dripping back into the ocean. He set her bare feet down on the dock and watched as she wrung out her white hair.

"Who do you think did it?" Nado asked, rubbing a piece of the plant between a finger and thumb, popping one of the bubbles in it's flesh and releasing a gush of watery, toxic slime. "A pirate would sooner stab the boy in the back than poison him, but then only a pirate would think to use cove grass in the first place."

"A pirate," Onra said. "Or someone trying to frame a pirate."

Nado frowned, then his eyes widened. "Jug."

She spat in a very un-priestess gesture and flung her braid over her shoulder. "I've never liked that man."

"But why?" Nado said more to himself than to her. Why kill the prince?

Onra answered his unspoken question. "To destabilize the monarchy. He must have been a loyal subject to Nazark all this time. A spy. And a clever one to gain Casimir's favour."

"But it doesn't destabilize the monarchy. Lumir still lives, and no one will protest Casimir legitimizing him after Mormir's death." Nado shook his head. "And besides, why frame me?"

"Because he needed you gone too," Onra said. "After losing his little boy do you think Casimir would let you leave Missky? No, he'll keep you close, ready to swoop in incase Lumir gets ill. But if your head rolls then there's no doctor to save Lumir."

"You think Jug will try to kill him too?" Nado asked.

"I think he already has, he just didn't realize it wouldn't work as fast on Lumir as it did on Momir."

Nado frowned, realization setting in. "He'd tell Casimir himself what the poison was, saying he found it in a saddle bag or something. My saddle bag, once I arrived and the guards took my horse. He didn't think I'd find the poison myself, not in time to save Lumir or Nadia."

"He knew the King wouldn't let you cut Momir open."

Nado smiled, taking his sister's face between his hands and planting a warm kiss on her forehead. "He didn't count on you."

Onra smiled back. "Or my magic."

Nado grabbed his sister by the waist and tossed her up onto Deer's back before climbing up behind her. "Or your magic."

Nado jerked the reins and sent Deer flying back toward Missky, hooves beating a melodic rhythm against the boards of the wharf.

There was blood on the stairs to the Deck. Nado began running as soon as he saw it, abandoning his staff to rattle against the floor. Onra ran close behind, her wet feet smacking against the tiles, leaving a trail of ocean water in her wake.

Heart pounding in his ears, Nado skidded to a halt in the open doors to the Deck. Momir lay exactly where they'd left him, untouched. Jug was a heap on the floor, limbs limp, face reflecting in a growing pool of his own blood.

When Nado saw Lumir, panting, knife in hand, leaning against the stone slab supporting his brother's corpse, he relinquished a sigh of relief.

"You're alive," Nado said.

Lumir looked up, seeing Nado and Onra for the first time.

"He tried to stab me." His voice was shaky and he could hardly take his eyes from the body at his feet. "He did stab me," Lumir whispered.

"What?" Nado pushed into the room, ignoring the blood that slowly turned the hem of his robes red. "Where?"

He began patting Lumir down before the boy could point to his chest. A small flap of his shirt was sliced through, hanging down and making a triangle window to his chest. The cut beneath was little worse than a scratch.

Onra, peering over Nado's shoulder, sighed with relief of her own. "Gods, he's fine."

"He tried to kill me," Lumir said.

"Yes," Nado said. "He likely realized framing me wasn't going to work anymore."

Thundering footsteps rang in the hall a moment before the King burst in with a retinue of guards in green and gold, weapons in hand. Behind them was one sheepish looking cadet carrying Nado's saddle bag.

"Lumir," Casimir puffed, running through the blood to embrace his son. "What happened?"

Nado stepped away, letting Onra explain as he retrieved his saddle bag from the cadet.

The cadet's chest heaved, all bare except

for the light vest, his brown skin coppery from days spent guarding the walls in the hot sun. "My apologies, doctor. It took a little more convincing than I imagined to get the stable hand to relinquish it to me, then I couldn't find you."

"They do take good care of my horses here," Nado said. "A little too good, perhaps."

The cadet smiled and saluted then turned toward Momir's corpse. Despite having no one's eyes on him but Nado's, the cadet gave the prince a solemn bow before leaving the Deck.

One Prince was dead, another dying.

Nado took a small stone bowl and pestle from his bag and set it on the table next to the bowl of stomach contents still sitting there. In the fresh bowl he squirted sap from the bubbles of the cove grass, adding his own herbs, berries, and powdered minerals and grinding them into an elixir, adding more sap to make the consistency just right. When he was done he brought the bowl and a small metal spoon to a shaken Lumir.

"My Prince," Nado said, handing the bowl and spoon to him.

Lumir looked up at the title, one that hadn't yet been granted to him. Casimir didn't protest. Instead the King nodded his head in silent thanks to Nado.

"There's more than enough for him and Nadia," Nado said. "Just a couple spoonfuls each. Then bedrest and lots of water. As a precaution."

"You'll stay in Missky?" Casimir said, his tone wavering on the cusp between question and demand.

Nado nodded. "Of course."

The King nodded and turned back to his eldest son, his only son.

Nado collected his tools and put them back into his bag before tossing it onto his shoulder. He looked back at Momir then, his small body not yet full grown, splayed out on a slab of rock. Sleeping, it was so easy to still picture him sleeping. In that moment the Deck became too crowded, too rancid with the smell of drying blood. Nado found the nearest door and stepped out into one of the many famed gardens of Missky.

Green hung from every ledge and sill. Grass grew tall beneath his boots. Flowers, flowers of every colour, grew wild on this tiny, untamed terrace.

Nado knelt by a patch of long stemmed blue roses surrounded by a variety of other blossoms. He picked one, snapping the stem. A thorn pricked his finger in the process and he watched as a bead of red blood trickled across his knuckle. He wiped it on his already soiled robe and watched as a fresh drop rose to the surface of his skin. How many such events just like this had his sister spared him over the years? A prick here, a scrape there.

Nado stood, jostling the saddle bag resting on his shoulder. A soft chime filled the terrace.

Nado twirled the blue rose between his fingers, watching the petals twirl, like a Nazark dancer. And such beautiful dancers they were, Nado had seen them on more than one occasion. Yet those same people ate the flesh of their dead, plotted the murder of a boy, and had seen it through.

Perspective, he mused. To some, green is as good as gold, pain worth the pleasure, a life worth a crown.

He looked back through the open doorway at his sister. Her back was to him as she spoke with the King and his son. Her tattoos were hidden by long sleeves that covered even her hands and her hair was still braided tightly down her back. Besides her sodden robes she looked like the perfect Missky priestess, and not at all his little pirate sister.

A shadow skirted the edge of the terrace, large dark wings circling ever lower.

Saljack cried only a moment before landing on Nado's offered forearm. Nado ground his teeth against the pain of the talons.

But he smiled at the bird, stroking the fine metallic feathers, wondering what magic the Priestesses and hawks shared that caused feathers and hair alike to appear aged.

Nado slipped another piece of salmon from the saddle bag on his shoulder, giving one end to Saljack and tugging at the other, not letting the bird have the food without a fight.

It didn't take Saljack long to rip the smoked meat from Nado's fingers and take his prize to the sky in a flurry of feathers. Nado watched his ascent, squinting against the setting sun before letting out a long breath and returning inside.

The Deck was empty then. People, people that weren't him, were uncomfortable around dead bodies. Jug's body remained as well, blood congealing on the tiles. Nado stepped forward and bent to shut his eyes. His own eyes flicked to the stab wound Lumir had inflicted in the man's ribs. Directly to the heart. A bastard had become a prince in that moment. And a boy, a man.

Jug had been with the royal family a long time, played to their beliefs, worshiped their gods. Nado wondered in his last moment if he'd thought about his afterlife and if he'd be rewarded for the murder of a prince, or if rather he feared the claws of Jokano.

Rising, Nado came to stand over Momir one last time. They would bury him in the morning, his body entombed in the Godskyi family mausoleum for the rest of time.

Nado looked at the rose still held tentatively between his fingers. Blue. Blue like Onra's robes, like tears, like the sea. He placed the rose on the boy's chest, careful not to let the thorns pierce his unmarred skin.

INDEBTED

Morris was sitting on his bunk, wondering if turning off the gravity in his chamber would make his mediation easier, or impossible, when he was interrupted by a shrill chime: a call from the bridge.

"You have a video call, Edward Morris." The AI pronounced his name in a mono-tone voice. Morris had meant to change that.

"Accept the call, Art."

It obeyed, and the screen on the wall above his bunk blinked to life, filling with the face of one of the GORRP fledglings.

"Captain Morris!" The thin, excitable man had his nose nearly pressed to the screen. "Captain, you've got to come quickly. He's out of his mind!"

"Who?"

"Creg!"

"What's he doing?"

"Just come—you must stop him!"

Morris sighed. "Fine. I'm on my way—Art, end call." The screen went black.

Morris got off his bunk and was almost to the coffee pot when the ship lurched, nearly knocking him off his feet.

"Art, make coffee."

"Yes, Edward Morris. I will make coffee."

The horrible voice made him grind his teeth, but there was no time to change it now. He made it to the door and then down the hall, stumbling as the ship continued to sway. He passed more GORRP fledglings—he really had to stop calling them that in case he accidentally said it out loud—scrambling in and out of their rooms, clinging to the walls to keep their feet under them.

By the time Morris made his way to the bridge it was a cacophony of beeps and alarms and the only people there were the panicked man who'd called him, and Creg, the pilot.

They'd picked Creg up at their last fuel stop when the pilot the GORRP had assigned them became ill. They'd left the old pilot on the planet to be collected when he was feeling better. Creg had been the last minute replacement. He was a Grand: an old, distinguished race, more typically known to be government advisors, royal administrators, or librarians. Morris hadn't thought to ask what one was doing on a remote planet working as a pilot-for-hire.

And he was regretting it right about now.

"Mr. Creg," Morris said to the large, white haired man occupying the pilot's chair. "Why is this ship rocking?"

"Birds," the man called back without turning to face Morris.

"Birds?"

"Big damn birds."

"We are in space, Mr. Creg. There are no birds—"

"He means the Varuth messenger ships, Captain Morris. They patrol this area as there have been many pirate raids lately and even brigands making—" the ship made a hard dive to the left, knocking the man to the floor. Morris helped him to his feet once the ship righted.

"—illegal landings. They just wanted to make routine contact. They didn't even request to board, but Creg just started running from them for no reason and now they're treating us as hostiles!"

"Creg, I want you to stop this ship immediately and make contact with the Varuth so we can work this out." Morris instructed.

"Can't."

Morris could feel his jaw tightening. "What do you mean, can't?"

"Can. Not."

"Captain, our ship can't go beyond .5c or else we won't have the fuel to get to Eohine."

Morris turned to the quivering man beside him. "Who are you?"

"An engineer," he replied.

"Is this radio capable of contacting the Varuth?" Morris asked, taking the headphones hanging around the GORRP's neck.

"Yes, sir."

Morris put them on and brought the mouth piece to his lips. "This is Captain Edward Morris, acting Sivy Commander aboard GORRP1039. We are not hostiles. I repeat, not hostiles—we are on a scientific expedition funded by the Government of the Reformed Republic Plilia. Our pilot mistook you for an enemy ship as he is unfamiliar with the area. I apologize for the confusion and ask that you relinquish pursuit. We will make contact and you are more than welcome to board."

There was only silence on the other end.

Morris tapped the head phones. "Are you sure this—"

The ship jolted to the right, throwing the

GORRP engineer to the floor with Morris right on top of him.

"Creg!" Morris shouted, pushing himself up.

"Not me."

"It's the Varuth. They're attacking!" the engineer cried, scrambling out from under Morris.

Morris closed his eyes and shoved a hand into his coat where his fingers found the little neon pink poker chip which he turned over and over inside his pocket. He tried to calm himself.

10, 9, 8...

Another series of what Morris assumed to be small missiles shook the ship.

7, 6, 5...

Small, but large enough to seriously damage the ship.

4, 3...

And if he didn't make it to Eohine, he was screwed.

"Creg. Get us out of here."

"The balls you think I've been doing over here?" Creg grumbled something else in his own tongue as Morris came up behind his chair.

"Can you out maneuver them?" Morris asked.

"Nope."

"What are you going to do then?"

"Out run them."

Morris felt the floor begin to hum beneath his boots. He watched the screens in front of Creg flashing and beeping hysterically. One in particular had numbers increasing so quickly he could barely make one out before it morphed into the next.

"Creg, is that our speed?"

Without looking at the dial Creg made a guttural noise Morris took as confirmation.

"But you heard the engineer, if you push us beyond .5c we won't make it to our destination."

"That's the two things that give me the shits—engineers and green apples."

"Excuse me?"

"Sit down and buckle up, you idiot."

Morris ignored the slight and did as instructed. "You." he said over his shoulder at the engineer, once he'd buckled himself into the seat beside Creg. "Go out there and tell everyone to get in their chambers and buckle in."

The man gave a vigorous nod and sprinted from the bridge.

Morris watched the screens that showed the sleek blue Varuth birds in close pursuit.

"What will you do when you outrun them?" Morris knew Creg couldn't shake them and make it to Eohine.

"If I out run them."

"What? You said you could."

The tall man shrugged his shoulders. "Probably can. Then we'll talk about next steps."

Morris closed his eyes again, reaching for his poker chip. He began the deep breathing exercise he'd read about in the used copy of 'Inner Peace for Mortals' he'd picked up at a bargain shop during their first fuel up. In through the nose, out through the mouth, lips pressed together. In, out. In, out...

"You praying?"

Morris opened his eyes. "What?"

The ship rocked again and Creg grunted as he swerved the ship away from a second blast. "I knew a man that prayed like that."

"I'm not praying."

"I'm not going to get you killed."

"I certainly hope not."

"Well you can cut out the praying then. It's distracting."

"I'm not...oh never mind." Brute.

The distance between them and the Varuth ships was growing. In a matter of minutes, which felt like hours, there was nothing but black space at their back.

Creg kept the ship at a break neck speed, but with their pursuers gone he flew it straight and steady. Morris tried to catch his breath without looking like he was doing so. He was supposed to be Captain of this ship, in control of it and its crew. Only he wasn't a military man. He was just a scientist. The title of Captain was temporary and unearned. A gesture on behalf of the GORRP who were the financial benefactors for the mission.

As the ship slowed to its normal speed Morris unbuckled.

"Let's talk next steps," he said, leaning over the console so he could look at Creg. He was older than Morris had originally thought, with deep pools in his cheeks and wrinkles around his eyes and nose. It was impossible to tell exactly how old he was. The Grands were one of the oldest races in the universe and could live for centuries.

"We're stopping at Yhit to refuel. Then

carrying on to Eohine," Creg said.

"Yhit is out of the way. If we go there to fuel up we won't get to Eohine before our deadline."

"And we won't get there at all if we don't fuel up." Creg stood, and Morris was forced to take a step back to still be able to see the man without looking straight up. Creg towered over him by at least two feet, his head nearly touching the roof of the ship.

Damn monsters.

"Who are you?" Morris asked.

"If I get you to Eohine, does it matter?"

Morris didn't reply. He watched Creg leave the bridge before he returned to his own chamber.

"The coffee is ready, Edward Morris," Art said as the doors slid open.

"Thank you, Art." Morris poured himself a cup from the percolator into one of the GORRP Enterprise mugs and returned to sitting cross legged on his bed.

10, 9, 8, 7...

Does Creg know I'm desperate to get to Eohine, or am I just reading into his brutish manner?

6, 5...

And if he does know, then how, and what does he want? How can he use my situation to his advantage?

4...3...

"Shit." Morris stood again and began to pace around his small room. He took the poker chip form his pocket, flipping it off his thumb then catching it repeatedly.

"Are you distressed, Edward Morris?" Art asked.

Yes! "No, Art. I'm fine."

Morris set down his mug and pulled out the chair from the small desk he'd just barely managed to squeeze into the corner of the room. Art sat on the desktop; a small, metal cube that remotely controlled everything in Morris's room. Granted, it was a small room, but Art was capable of controlling much larger areas—and a lot of other things that didn't necessarily belong to Morris.

Morris looked down at the little pick poker chip with an image of silver eye in its center. Creg was right, it didn't matter at all who he was, so long as he got Morris to Eohine in the next four days.

As Morris was being crammed into the stiff ferry seats, harnessed in with at least eight different belts and clips, he was reminded that Creg was a giant. The man, seated next to him, couldn't help but take up more than his fair share of space. Even with his arms crossed his right arm pressed against Morris' shoulder. Morris turned his face away to avoid having his cheek plastered to the man's bicep.

By the time the ferry touched down on Eohine, Morris had a knot in his neck and had lost all feeling in his left arm.

"Those seats were designed for little people," Creg said as he followed Morris and three of the GORRP fledglings—employees—into the Eohine Customs center.

Morris turned to look at him. "You could have stayed on the spaceport. Your presence is unnecessary down here."

Creg shrugged. "I flew your but here, might as well see what all the hurry was about."

Morris still had no idea how Creg had gotten them to Eohine in four days. Fuel up's typically took at least a day. Half that time was just waiting for a fueling team to become available. Apparently Creg knew people in high places, or low places more likely, and he got them fueled and back on route in less than six hours.

The little engineer looked at him like he was a God, evidently forgetting the near brush with death Creg had earned them with the Varuth. Morris was just thankful the episode hadn't been repeated.

The Customs center was a white, dome-like building. All smooth sides, it rose into the sky like a wave, back dropped by the white tipped mountains in the distance. They were led to a welcome desk by the ferry pilot, where they were instructed to hand over their papers.

Morris and his team obliged, but Creg, being a last minute recruit and not actually assigned by the GORRP, didn't have papers proving he was a part of their scientific expedition.

The dark, lanky secretary behind the desk curled her poppy red hair around a finger while she listened patiently to Morris' explanation.

"Not a problem," she said sweetly when he'd finished. "I'll just have to run a quick search, and as long as nothing pops up, he's fee to join you."

She scanned Creg's face and profile with a

blue light from a small gadget on her desk before poking away at the screen in front of her.

Morris turned to Creg. "Please tell me you don't have a warrant or something, because I swear to—"

"Looks good Dr. Morris. He's clear to go on through."

Creg didn't acknowledge Morris' half-finished accusation. They collected their papers from the secretary and moved on. Morris asked a passing Customs personnel where he could find the Exploratory Prep center and then followed his instructions to a small changing room at the back of the building. He and the GORRP employees immediately started undressing.

"What are we doing?" Creg asked, a little startled.

"We have to make sure we have nothing that will contaminate the planet. Strip down, put your things in one of the boxes, take a shower."

Creg looked skeptically at the clear plastic boxes lining the far wall. They were in a long tube that would automatically clean their clothes and belongings and deposit them into a room on the far side of the showers.

"Or go back and wait on the ship," Morris said, noticing Creg's hesitation.

Creg looked at him defiantly, then began undressing.

The GORRP were the first ones in the shower, Morris close on their heels. Creg wasn't even out of his pants yet when Morris turned just before getting in the shower to call back to him.

"Oh, and try to hold your breath in the showers, you don't want any of these chemicals up your nose. Bad enough they're getting in our pours."

He left a slightly distressed looking Creg and stepped into the showers.

Eohine was stranger then Morris had imagined. The forests were dense but almost no two trees looked alike to the untrained eye. Their shape and colours competed in what seemed an utterly random array of species. It was a jungle unlike any other Morris had ever been in.

Creg was having a hard time keeping up.

"These blasted branches keep hitting me in the face," Creg complained. He had to perpetually duck to maneuver through the trees unhampered.

"Could have stayed on the ship," Morris

repeated for the tenth time.

"What are you tree huggers even looking for out here?"

"A flower," Morris said. "A little purple flower. Very small, very rare. Don't trod on it."

Creg looked at his feet; his large boots left deep, distinct prints in the soft, almost powdery soil.

"How will we find it in this mess if it's so small?" he asked.

"You'll smell it," Morris said. "You'll smell it a mile away. Like sour-croute. You ever had sour-croute?"

Creg shook his head.

"Well, you're in for a treat."

They split ways then. Morris had photocopies of a rudimentary map of Eohine. He'd shaded in a different section on each map, marking the areas he wanted to be searched. He gave one to each of his team and sent them off. Then, Creg in tow, he set off to search his own area.

38 degrees Celsius. Zero cloud cover, Art informed him. Morris had a small com in his right ear so that Art could relay Eohine's climate stats and monitor his own vitals. It always paid to be careful in environments as unknown as

Eohine's.

As they walked through the thick forest, Morris noticed some of the leaves already turning; the outer edges a darker colour then the middles. Some looked like they'd been dipped in blue or pink paint, creating a hypnotic illusion when they grew too close the ground, disrupting Morris' perception of depth, making the ground look like it was slithering beneath his feet.

Creg stumbled on behind him.

Good thing we aren't looking for a critter, Morris thought. He'll have scared off everything in a ten mile radius.

"Why?" Creg asked as they passed a clear blue stream, likely running down from the mountains. "Why did you come all this way for a flower?"

"Its petals, when ground into a paste, may produce a chemical with enormous healing properties," Morris said.

"May? Meaning it may not?"

Morris shrugged. "I found notes from one of the original colonization parties while doing research for a bio-tech firm—"

"Jargon, man."

"Someone who originally colonized the

planet found the flower and, for some reason they didn't care to specify in their personal notes, believed it had extraordinary healing properties."

"And the GORRP sent you half way across the galaxy for what may or may not be a magic flower?"

Morris hesitated. "I sort of implied that there was more evidence to support its legitimacy."

"And is there?"

Morris didn't respond. He ducked under a particularly low arching branch.

"I'll take that as a no." Creg had to bend double to get under the branch. "Why the deadline then?"

"What do you mean?"

"You took a gamble on a dead man's diary and you had to get here right away? Were you just eager to see how badly you screwed yourself of what?"

"The flower has a limited life cycle," Morris explained. "Eohine inhabits a binary star system. For the flower to bloom the twin stars must be in perfect solar alignment, and alignment must occur during Eohine's wet season."

"And how often do both those things happen?"

40 degrees Celsius.

"Every ten years," Morris said. "And that's if the season is wet enough. It needs a lot of moisture to grow."

"And all this info was in this guy's notebook, yet he failed to mention exactly how effective the flower juice is?"

"No. Some of it was there, only speculation, of course. They knew very little about the planet other than what they gathered from the natives. The rest I managed to figure out by comparing the sketches of the flower to similar species in other binary systems—I have a degree in botany so—"

"Natives?"

"Yes, there were and still are Native Eohines. Because of the drastic and unique climates Eohine is a protected planet. Colonization was limited only to the small area surrounding the Customs center."

"Are these Natives—"

"Don't move!" Morris threw a hand behind him, placing a hand against Creg's chest, for all the good it would do. It would hardly be a barrier to a man like Creg, but he stopped anyway.

Morris sniffed. The smell wasn't very strong, but it was their; a faint tarte aroma that tickled the nostrils.

"Art, temperature."

44 degrees Celsius.

That shouldn't be hot enough, but...

"Humidex?"

48 degrees Celsius.

Morris scanned the ground in front of him. It had become softer the farther they'd gone into the forest. Hardly any light shone through the dense canopy. Patches of soil were covered in a bright orange moss.

He got on his hands and knees and carefully started pushing aside feather-like leaves to inspect the ground beneath.

"The flower will grow under the shade of one of these plants."

"Morris..."

"It's fickle because it needs so much sun yet only grows where almost no sun can reach it. That's why this time of year is so important."

"Morris, those natives you mentioned—"

Morris brushed aside a particularly large leaf, its veins a vibrant blue, almost human like.

Beneath was a small, purple flower with petals the shape of perfect spades. Morris hastily took a small resalable plastic bag from his belt and put the flower inside neatly. His heart was beating fast, so fast it blocked out the noise of footsteps until a branch snapped right in front of him. He looked up and found his nose almost brushing the tip of an arrow head.

He didn't have time to analyze the man behind the bow before a sharp twinge in his right shoulder had his vision swimming.

Wound detected.

It became hard to breath, and the wet air didn't make it any easier.

Edward Morris, I have detected a harmful substance entering the bloodstream. Hydration would be advisable.

A swell of nausea rose up in his throat. He thought he could hear someone scream behind him, but blood was pumping too loudly in his ear drums.

49 degrees Celsius.

Morris fell forward and retched into a nearby bush.

Are you distressed, Edward Morris?

Yes!

Morris collapsed face first into the wet,

Eohine earth.

The dreams were almost worse than the nausea.

Surely Creg paid the Natives to do me in. In fact, the GORRP probably paid Creg. The old captain hadn't gotten sick; he'd faked it so they could sneak an assassin on board. Why pay me all those lovely royalties for the drug when they could put one down payment on a thug and cut out their middle man? I already know how to use the flower, but it isn't rocket-science. Any other biologist with half a wit could figure it out, and many would do it for less money than the GORRP's promised me...

Morris licked his dry, cracked lips. That's when he realized he was alive, and about to be sick.

He sat up and vomited over the side of the table he'd been laying on. He was staring down at blue and green tiles, now splattered with his stomach contents. He licked his lips again and looked up. Creg was sitting in a chair much too small for him in the corner of the Exploration Prep room. Steam from the nearby showers filled the edges of the room.

"What happened?" Morris asked when he was sure he'd emptied his stomach.

"Natives," Creg said.

"I remember that much," Morris said harshly. He noticed then that he was naked.

Where's the flower?

"I have it," Creg said, noting the panic come over Morris features.

"Where?" Morris slid off the table.

"Right here." Creg took the small bag from a pocket in his double breasted jacket.

Morris snatched it from his fingers.

"Ungrateful Earthling," Creg muttered.

Morris' clothes were folded at the end of the table. He hesitantly put the flower down long enough to dress. His eye's never left the bag.

"What happened with the Natives?" Morris asked.

"They shot you."

Morris rubbed his shoulder. There was a large piece of gauze tapped to his arm. No sign of blood though, and only a dull ache, like after receiving a vaccination.

"How'd we get back?"

"I tossed one of the little sprites into a tree. That bought me enough time to through you over my shoulder and get out of there. They chased me all the way out of the forest, blowing their little darts at me."

"Darts? Is that what shot me?"

Creg nodded. "The white coat said those darts are poisoned, but you'll live. They cause hallucinations and paranoia, but he figured he spared you the worst of it."

Paranoia. Morris slipped the flower into the zipper pocket on the front of his right thigh and checked to make sure his poker chip was still in his pocket. Then he put his ear piece back in so he could hear Art.

Hello, Edward Morris. Did you sleep well?

Morris ignored Art. "Alright, well that was enough excitement for one day. Let's go."

Creg stood and led the way out of the Exploration Prep room. Morris followed, a little unsteadily behind him. They were almost at the secretary's desk when Creg made a hard right down a side hallway.

"Hey, where are you going?" Morris said, hurrying to catch up.

"I need to find someone."

"What? Who?" Morris shook his head. "No, never mind. I don't care. We just need to get off this planet."

"I'll only be a few minutes."

"I'm in charge of this crew and you have to do as I say if you want to see any sort of compensation."

Creg grunted.

Morris ground his teeth. "I have been abused by Natives and almost had my entire mission wrecked—"

Creg spun around. "And those Natives would have made a merry ol' hog roast out of you had I not dragged your drooling ass out of there, so how about you give me a few minutes?"

Morris shut his mouth. It was hard to feel superior to Creg with the man looming over him.

Creg returned to his march down the hallway.

Who is this man? Morris watched him for a moment before deciding to stay with him. It would be easier to keep an eye on him that way.

Morris had to walk twice as fast to keep up with Creg's long strides.

"What is that?" Morris asked when he noticed Creg holding a small card. He was apparently using it as a reference; looking at it before poking his head into a doorway.

"Photo."

Morris tried to get a better look. "A girl? You're here looking for a girl? Don't you have any of those back on your planet?"

Creg didn't respond. He kept stopping in doorways, looking around at the faces, and then moving on.

Morris sighed. "This place is massive. Let me see that."

He took the picture from Creg and removed Art from his pants pocket. He pushed one of the small buttons on the side of the cube so Creg could hear Art as well.

"Art, scan."

"Scanning, Edward Morris," the cube replied, sending out a yellow light that took in the picture.

Creg raised an eyebrow. "Why does its voice sound like someone's got it by the gonads?"

Morris sighed. "I'm working on it."

"Scan complete."

"Art, use Eohine's security system to see if you can find a match to the scan."

The cube hummed. "You do not have permission to access Eohine's network."

"Ask nicely."

The cube hummed again, then little blue lights starting flashing along its sides to show that it was processing.

Creg raised an eyebrow. "Ask nicely?"

Morris didn't respond to the implied question. Creg didn't need to know it was code for 'hack the system'.

"Match found in Common Room C."

"Directions?"

"Turn left twice. Common Room C is the first door on the right side, indicated on the network map by a blue sphere and three red stars."

Morris looked at Creg. "As in the sigil of the Talverian Military? What business do you have with Talveria?"

"Talveria: recently fought in the Larameen conflict. Lost 26 of their stations to the United Due Force, making their last stand for the solar system on Hive planet Ruman. Were ultimately pushed out. Now intergalactic refugees."

"Thank you, Art." Morris said. "They're outcasts right now. No one wants them."

"I'm returning something to one of their soldiers." Creg walked off, following the instructions Art gave them with no further explanation.

The Common Room had become a temporary military base, likely a barracks for some of the scattered Talverian soldiers. It wasn't active, Eohine didn't allow military action to be hosted on planet, but you wouldn't know that from the look of the occupants.

The tall, red skinned Talverian were all in their uniforms. Trim, slate-gray trousers and angular jackets that buttoned diagonally across the chest. Some of the lower ranking soldiers wore bomber jackets instead. It was one of the later that Creg went over to.

"Lotus Omans?" Creg asked.

The young female Talverian turned around; she'd been slipping sleek metal bracers over the long black cuffs of her jacket.

"I am," she replied.

"My name is Creg, I..." Morris watched as Creg seemed to shrink before the tiny Talverian girl. His shoulders hunched and his head bowed in an almost sheepish gesture.

"I was there when your brother fell. Captain Omans was a brave man. He stayed behind on his ship, alone, so that the rest of his battalion could flee. None of them would have lived had he not remained."

The girl's large black eyes looked up at him. She appeared totally unaware of how he dwarfed her. "You saw him fall?"

Creg nodded.

"You killed him?"

Hesitantly, Creg nodded again.

The girl nodded back, like she had expected nothing less. Some of the other Talverians who'd been listening stiffened, some of them grabbing their own metal bracers, or hands going to the weapons on their belts. Morris wished he hadn't come in with Creg. He put his hands in his pockets, taking a step back and hoping that if a fight broke out he wouldn't be associated with Creg.

Creg unfastened three of the buttons on his coat and slipped off a ribbon he'd been wearing around his neck. The medallion that it carried had been hidden beneath his coat. Morris knew why. A piece of gold that size was worth a small fortune, not to mention the detail of the workmanship probably made it valuable to collectors.

"I didn't want to shoot him in the end, when I saw his bravery, but he was determined to go down with his vessel. I don't believe he had any plans to leave there alive. I know that's not an excuse, so I thought I owed him at least this."

Creg handed the medallion to the girl, who accepted and clutched it to her chest.

"Thank you." Her words were little more than a whisper.

Creg nodded again then saluted, a large hand pressed diagonally across his chest. By the way the Talverian responded, Morris guessed it was a gesture of her people and not his.

Creg left the room then, Morris on his heels.

"What was that?" Morris asked.

"A death medal."

"A death medal?"

"A talisman given to Talverian youth when they join the military sector," Art provided. "It is to be kept with them at all times. They believed that upon death the essence of the person goes into the medal. The medals of deceased soldiers are displayed in the home in shrines called Soul Crypts."

"Creepy," Morris muttered. "But that was really nice, what you did for that girl. It must mean a lot to her family."

Creg didn't say anything.

"You could have sold it you know. It would have cost a fortune—"

"The war was about money," Creg said. "But his death wasn't. His death was about saving lives."

"Mr. Creg!"

Creg and Morris had nearly reached the ferry dock when Lotus' call stopped them. The young woman jogged down the hallway, her brother's medal still in her hands.

"Mr. Creg I just wanted to thank you again. This really does mean so much to me. And that you would come here among all these Talverian soldiers...I've been posted, I'm leaving Eohine tomorrow. Did you know that?"

Creg nodded. "I almost missed you. If it hadn't been for Captain Morris taking me on I never would have reached Eohine in time."

Lotus turned to Morris with a wide smile.

"Okay, great," Morris said, uncomfortable with finding himself the center of attention. "I'm glad you two worked this out, but I too am on a tight schedule so can we please get moving?"

"I'll ride up with you," Lotus said. "I want to hear about the last battle my brother fought."

Morris sighed but didn't protest the woman's joining them.

He clambered into the ferry seats yet again, squished between Creg and Lotus. The trip back to Eohine's space port was just as uncomfortable as their ride to the planet and this time it was accompanied by a constant slew of questions from Lotus. Creg answered in his customary way by using as few syllables as possible, but Lotus refused to let him leave out a single detail.

When the ferry docked, Morris swallowed his nausea and managed to squirm out between the two of them, getting off the ferry first. Creg lingered, saying goodbye to Lotus. Morris stretched his legs while he waited, relieved he'd be spending the rest of his journey home on a much larger craft then the ferry.

The ship the GORRP had supplied him with wasn't large compared to most cargo or battle ships, but it was big for Eohine. The majority of the other vessels were smaller crafts; a long tourist ship, a few personal cruisers, a couple sleek blue birds.

Birds...

Morris hit the deck, literally, just as a couple shots rang over his head, each one sounding like a miniature sonic boom.

I've detected hostiles, Edward Morris.

No shit.

Morris rolled himself under a nearby cruiser just as two Varuth pilots darted around the corner of the bay. They obviously hadn't seen Morris get into his hiding spot, but they had no problem spotting Creg. Lotus already had her own weapon in her hands. She stepped in front of Creg and aimed at the Varuth.

"Put down your weapons. You are on Eohine territory. Eohine is a neutral planet. You are required by—"

Creg grabbed her shoulders and spun around, pulling her to his chest and he did so. He took a blast to the back, knocking them both forward. Lotus slipped out of his arms and fired off two, quick shots, downing both of the Varuth with stunning accuracy.

Creg had fallen to the ground, and he wasn't moving.

Morris rolled out from under the cruiser and ran to Creg. Lotus was already kneeling beside him, her weapon still in hand.

"Is he alright?" Morris asked.

Lotus nodded. "He's breathing. Why were those Varuth shooting at you?"

Morris cringed. "It's a long story."

"Well there are several birds here which means more than just these two Varuth. You two need to get out of here."

"Creg is our pilot," Morris said, watching a deep violet puddle of blood forming beneath the man's left side.

"What about your co-pilot?"

"We don't have one. We're only small scientific vessel."

"Can't you fly, Captain?"

"I'm just a biologist."

Lotus sighed. "Very well, I'll fly. I owe him one. Get him to his feet, we need to move."

Morris looked down at the giant man lying on his back on the dock. Getting him on his feet would be easier said than done. He took Art from his pocket and slipped him into Creg's pocket instead.

"Art, give him a jolt, something safe. I need him walking. And run his vitals."

There was zap and Creg's eyes flew open. He gasped.

"Hey, welcome back. I need you to walk."

"What happened? Lotus?"

"She's fine. She's getting us to the ship, hopefully without getting shot." Morris helped him stand, slipping under his arm to support him as they made their way towards the ship.

"What bay?" Lotus asked.

"Nine."

She ran ahead, weapon held down by her thigh.

The whole port was alive with alarms and lights now. Personal were running between bays, but none of them seemed armed. A few gave Morris and Creg a hesitant glance as they ran by, but the trail of blood they were leaving behind them seemed to scare away any questions. Still, Morris wished Lotus hadn't gone ahead.

"You have a weapon?" Morris asked Creg.

"Yes."

"Let me have it then."

"No."

"No? The Varuth could attack us again at any moment."

"I'll take my chances. You're liable to blast your own foot off. Or mine"

Morris didn't have time to dispute as they nearly ran into a Varuth sprinting around the corner. He was just as surprised as Morris and that gave Lotus enough time to shoot him in the back as she appeared at the end of the hall, just outside bay nine.

The Varuth crumpled, his weapon crashing to the floor.

"Nice timing," Morris said.

Lotus took Creg's other side and together they got him on the ship. Morris laid him down on the floor of the bridge. They'd have time to get him into a bed once they were safely away from Eohine.

The crew was scrambling.

"The Varuth are back!" the engineer hollered as he came running onto the bridge.

"I'm aware," Morris grumbled. "Is everyone on board?"

The engineer nodded.

"Good, tell them to sit down and shut up until we get this thing moving."

The engineer left in just as much of a panic as he'd entered.

"This is bigger than I've ever flown," Lotus said. She was sitting in the pilot's seat, her dainty red hands flying over the control board.

"Can you do it?"

"Maybe."

"Art, get into the ships system and help Lotus fly us out of here."

A moment later the ship hummed to life.

"I will run the novice flight guide for this model craft, if you have any inquiries..." Art's voice cut out as Lotus threw on a flight headset.

Morris returned his attention to Creg. He was unconscious again, more blood pooling on the floor. He wasn't a doctor, but luckily he'd taught Art to multi task.

"Art, how is he?"

His heart rate is slowing drastically. Art said into his ear piece. Immediate medical attention is highly recommended.

"Not an option. How long does he have?"

At the current speed of his degradation, his heart will continue beating for approximately six minutes.

I need more time...

"How is he?" Lotus asked. Her attention was still firmly on the ship. Morris could hear the blasts of Varuth guns against the closed ship doors as they took off. It wouldn't be long until they got in their own ships and followed.

"Fine," Morris lied. "Art, what are our options?"

I'm afraid I have no sufficient alternatives to a medical professional.

Morris shut his eyes tight.

Though I would suggest the possibility of the flower—

"I know!"

Morris got to his feet and ran to his room. He pulled a silver case from under his bunk, then paused. He pulled the poker chip from his pocket. After a short consideration he didn't have time for, he placed the chip on the desk and sprinted back to the bridge.

"How long does he have now?"

Four minutes.

Morris skidded back onto the bridge and opened the case beside Creg. He removed a small mortar and pestle, a vial of concentrated minerals diluted in purified water, and biodegradable gauze. Then he took the small plastic baggie from his pants pocket.

He looked at the tiny purple flower, said a silent curse, then opened the bag and put the flower into the mortar. He crushed it into something resembling a moist powder, added the mineral water, then waited for it to combine. A sour aroma filled the ship.

One minute.

He hastily soaked the gauze in the liquid then stripped off Creg's coat and shirt and shoved the gauze into the open wound in his side. Morris gaged as his fingers squished into the exposed flesh, pushing out a wave of fresh blood.

He waited anxiously as Art monitored Creg's shallow breathing, checking for any improvement.

"How are we?" Morris asked Lotus.

"They were on my tail but I think I lost them."

Morris nodded. "Thank you."

"Where are you headed?"

"It doesn't matter. Stop at the next safe port and you can find a ride back to Eohine."

"You'll be out of a pilot."

"I'll figure it out." Morris picked up the bowl, looking at the little that was left of the mixture.

I'll have bigger problems then lack of a pilot.

He is improving. Heart rate is normal.

His eyes were opening then. His breathing still sounded wheezy, but he managed to speak.

"Lotus?"

"She's alright," Morris said. "She took your job though."

Creg tried to sit up, but Morris placed a hand on his chest. "You're going to want to wait."

Creg relented. He relaxed against the floor of the bridge, and then sniffed.

"What's that?"

"That is the smell of me saving your life."

"It smells like shit."

Morris laughed.

Lotus removed her headset and came to kneel beside Creg. She brushed his blonde hair out of his eyes with her long red fingers.

"I didn't mean to put you in danger," Creg said.

"You saved me. I think your debt to my brother has been paid in full."

Creg smiled and then looked to Morris.

"You used that dumb flower to save me?"

"Not so dumb now, is it?"

"The GORRP will want their money back."

Morris laughed bitterly. "They'll have to get in line."

"Was the flower very valuable?" Lotus asked, her wide dark eyes taking in the mortar and its milky-blue contents.

Morris stood. "The flower has medical properties that could help a lot of people. The contract was more valuable to me though. Another gamble."

"I'm sorry—"

Morris interrupted Creg. "The expedition was always about the money. But it didn't have to be."

Lotus stood too and began plotting their course to somewhere safe, while Morris left the bridge to find crew to help him get Creg into a bed.

Morris stared out at the green, picturesque waters Distad was famous for. The planet was a series of tropical islands surrounded by shallow emerald waters. It was a tourist trap and a customs nightmare. Even if the Varuth had managed to tail them, they would be hard pressed to find an excuse for docking their military cruisers at a tropical getaway.

The long windows running the length of the ship made for a perfect observatory of the ocean. The rest of the crew was indulging in Distad's delicacies while they waited to fuel up, but Morris had stayed on the ship. He wasn't in the mood for exotic tastes, even if he could have afforded them.

The ship doors slid open behind him and Creg, still moving slowly from his injuries, came to stand at his side.

"Did Lotus manage to find a ride?" Morris asked.

Creg nodded. There was a silence.

"She's very pretty," Morris said.

Creg turned a narrow glance on him.

Morris put up his hands in innocence. "I was thinking of you, of course. Not myself. Women cost too much."

Creg snorted. "We'll keep in touch." He didn't elaborate further on their relationship and Morris didn't push the issue.

"Did you find a pilot for me?"

"I'll fly."

"You're still healing—"

"I can fly. I'm not dying." Then he added, almost hesitantly: "Thanks to you."

Creg studied the green waves rolling beneath them for a moment before he turned toward the bridge.

Morris wasn't long in leaving too. He went to his room, laid down on his bed, and half-heartedly began counting before giving it up entirely and deciding to try and get some sleep before they took off again.

"Edward Morris?"

Morris sighed and rolled over, burying his face in the pillow. "What?" he mumbled.

"Miss Lotus left you a gift. She asked me to tell you about it."

Morris lifted his head and looked to his desk. On the corner, just beside Art's silver body, was a small package. His poker chip had been placed on top of it, the neon pink plastic sitting in the center of the brown paper.

Morris sat up and took the package, unwrapping it on his knees. Inside was a note and the death medal of Lotus' brother. The note read:

Talverians believe that the souls of departed soldiers are housed in these medals, which is why they are so important. But, Talverian's also hold to another belief, one I think to be more important; there are only so many types of souls and when we die we live on in all the other individuals who share our same soul. My brother's soul was that of a selfless man, who put the lives of others before his own. You've shown that you share a soul with my brother, and because of that, I gift this medal to you, to do with as you will. You have more use of it than my brother will anyways.

Thank you, and many blessings.   *– Lotus*

"Are you distressed, Edward Morris?"

"No. Why?"

"You are crying."

"Happy tears, Art." Morris sighed, smiling, and put the note back on his desk. "Art, look up traditional Talverian gifts of thank you."

Art's lights flashed blue. "Flowers are the most tradition form of apology or thanks in Talverian culture."

"Flowers, huh? Good. I have a new debt to pay."

A NOTE FROM THE AUTHOR

I've written these stories over many years. Some are new, some are old, but each has held a special place in my heart, and in my Word documents, waiting to see the light and to be put into the hands of a reader just like you.
You can't know what it means to me to have you read these words and walk these worlds, but it makes this author's heart glad. So thank you.

If you're looking for more stories, perhaps ones about grumpy naval officers rescuing their niece's lover who's lost at sea, or maybe a story about a young wizard and a spunky witch who fight demons together, or if space marines and cyberpunk nuns are more to your liking, then come find me on Instagram @mckaylaeaton.author to find more of my books and discover what new stories I'm working on.

Made in United States
Orlando, FL
23 June 2023

34445630R00189